LIVING SPRING

DIVORAN LITES

Real Life Books & Media

329 Cheney Highway #230

Titusville, FL 32780

www.rebekahlynbooks.com

Publisher's Note: This is a work of fiction. Some places and stories were inspired by real events, but have been changed to suit the needs of story. Names, characters, and incidents are a product of the author's imagination. Locales and public names are sometimes used for atmospheric purposes. Any resemblance to actual people, living or dead, or to businesses, companies, events, institutions, or locales is completely coincidental.

Living Spring/ DiVoran Lites

ISBN: 978-0-9965926-8-0

Mixed media painting by DiVoran Lites, Watercolor Impressions

Cover design by Laura of www.llpix.com

ACKNOWLEDGMENTS

No book is an island. If you go back to all the people who have told their stories, all the books you've ever read, the experiences you've had, the scenes you've seen; the number of people involved is almost exponential

Thanks to Ron Spangler for keeping our computer up and running for over twenty-five years and for holding our hands when we are in distress or despair about our lack of knowledge when it comes to technology. Thanks to him for being a ready reference on items of law-enforcement and crime.

Thanks to our daughter, Charlene Spangler for her gentle and quiet support and her endlessly patient help whenever we have questions about how to get the most out of Microsoft Word and Google.

Thanks to William David Lites, our son, for sharing his vast and fascinating knowledge of Florida, its environment, and its flora and fauna and for his kindness and generosity of spirit toward us in every possible way.

Thanks to Lisa Lites for her sweetness, encouragement, support, and respect. Thanks to her for open-handedly sharing her wonderful children all their lives.

Thanks to Jacob and Lacey Lites for making me happy, for their wisdom, and for keeping me young enough that I have a clue about how the younger generation thinks and feels in these times.

Thanks to friends from: Rebekah Lyn Books, and to Alta Young and Pam Gheen who make writing so much more fun and productive in every way.

Thanks to Beth Lynne for her wonderful editing, and to Laura of www.llpix.com for her handling of my cover paintings for the Florida Springs Trilogy.

That is by no means all the people to whom I owe thanks; I hope you know who you are and how much I appreciate you.

Most of all, of course, thanks to God. Where would I be without him? It doesn't bear thinking about.

God places the lonely in families…
Psalm 68:6, New Living Translation (NLT)

To Bill, and Lisa, Ron and Charlene, Lacey, and Jacob.
Thank you, my dears, for being my immediate family.

CHAPTER 1

My name is Jean Schaefer. I'm a finance major who is helping my brother Hank and his wife run the business we inherited when our parents died, and I'm a single mother as well. It's difficult to know when something actually starts, but I will begin with the evening I pulled into the graveled parking lot of the Crossroads Mercantile and Gas, wishing Missy and I had arrived earlier in the day.

The store was a dilapidated building wedged between huge trees that dripped with Spanish moss. It looked like something from a gothic horror movie. It was already giving me the willies and I hadn't even gone inside yet. All that remained of the paint was a few streaks of dirty white, barely visible against the weathered clapboards. Posts supported the sagging porch roof, but so poorly, I feared that it would collapse if even a mockingbird landed on it.

My daughter, Missy, who was four years old, was in that hungry-sleepy state where all she could do was whine. I tried to maintain my patience despite being exhausted and emotionally drained from the strain of closing up our home. It had been such a haven in my recent bout with agoraphobia.

I'd been seeing a therapist and she said I was suffering from Post Traumatic Stress Disorder, that bugaboo of many a wartime vet. It also affects people like me, who find themselves in life and death situations. I'm better now, though; Missy and I are planning some drastic changes in our lives.

Today, I had I stalled until the last minute to pack, then signed papers, and now we were hot, tired, hungry, and running late—not that anyone was waiting—but the sky was growing darker by the moment. What could we expect? Summer was over and daylight savings time had flown. We probably should have stopped at a supermarket on the way, but I was afraid to get off the Interstate for fear of getting lost.

It didn't help when the car radio segued from a romantic Beethoven sonata to a dark piece by Mahler. As I snapped it off, I heard a host of cicadas buzzing in the branches overhead. Crickets sawed and frogs peeped. There had to be a black lagoon around somewhere, along with the creature that would crawl out and get us.

"Missy, tell Mother not to be silly," I said as I adjusted the rear view mirror so I could see her car seat in the back. As always, gazing upon her sweet face gave me a moment of peace. She had red curls like mine, but instead of green eyes, she had inherited her father's bright brown ones. Too bad he hadn't stuck around long enough to watch her grow up.

"Mommy, don't be silly," she parroted, the way I had trained her to.

"You're right. I've got to calm down." Taking a deep breath and holding it for the count of seven, I started the relaxation technique Dr. Louise had taught me and soon felt able to open the car door. A bird somewhere in the undergrowth sounded off. *Chuck-will-widda.*

"What's that bird?" Missy demanded. Elaine, my naturalist sister-in-law, had taught Missy to ask questions about the flora and fauna in order to help me stay focused.

"That's a chuck-will's-widow, sweetheart." For her sake, I tried to sound calm and courageous. It helped a little. "We'd better go in. There's barely time to get everything we need before they close: I touched the tips of my fingers and listed, "Hot dogs, buns, milk, and cereal." I got out of the car and went to the back seat, where I unbuckled Missy's straps.

"And animal crackers for Missy," my daughter counted off. "Camels, elephants, and bears."

It was then that I heard the *whee* sound of another kind of bird and looked up. A large raptor soared through a break in the trees, and my heart lifted to see it flying wild. It had something long and wiggly dangling from its talons, though, and a shiver ran up my back.

Snakes! I didn't think study would help me get over my abhorrence of them. This area had several poisonous ones, such as rattlesnakes, copperheads, cottonmouth moccasins, and coral snakes. An explosion from a gun made my body jerk involuntarily and I saw the big bird plummet into a thicket nearby. As soon as I could move, I picked Missy up and ran for the store.

Under more pleasant circumstances, I might have enjoyed the typically old-fashioned sights and smells of a general store. The clean aroma of laundry soap relieved a fusty-musty odor of rotting burlap that lay under the tang of coffee beans and a whiff of slightly sour milk.

I inhaled the distinct scent of leather from a saddle, with its stirrups dangling, that had been thrown over a sawhorse. The unmistakable smell left behind by generations of mice permeated everything. I assumed the grain that seeped into the cracks between the boards from sacks piled on the floor was chicken feed, but I was sure the mice liked it too. There were mysterious-looking bins and rows of overloaded shelves crowding the aisles.

Amid the clutter, Missy discovered a bucket of fluorescent plastic fishing worms and began happily lining them up nose-to-tail across the gritty floor. Oh, well, she'll get a bath when we arrive at the house, I thought.

Picking my way around displays of mosquito repellent and suntan lotion, I ducked under a rack of corncob pipes and nearly fell over a stack of tobacco tins. The only thing missing was a clerk. I located the cash register and headed toward it, thinking that surely someone would be there.

"Hello?" I called, looking down the long counter toward the back of the store.

"Hey there!" a large middle-aged clerk in a flowered housedress popped up from under the counter in front of me. I jumped back and took another deep breath, wondering again how my nerves would ever hold up under country living.

"Sorry I startled you, miss." She was gray-haired, and had a streak of dirt across her cheek. "I been cleanin'." She dusted her hands together as if to demonstrate her industriousness. "What can I do for you?"

"Somebody just shot a big bird out there. Do they let people run around with guns, shooting whatever they want?" I didn't realize I was actually wringing my hands until I saw her staring; then I stopped and stuffed them in the pockets of my twill skirt.

"Sure, it's illegal, but they think its okay as long as they don't get caught. Their daddies and granddaddies always shot whatever they wanted, so now them boys think they can too." She shook her head with disgust.

"Shouldn't we do something…report it?" I asked.

"Now looky here. You just forget it," she said. "We don't want to make them boys mad. It surely in't nothing much but a old hawk. It's not a eagle; you can get in big trouble for shooting one of those. Now what can I get you?"

I didn't like the way she dismissed the terrible thing that had just happened, but I was a stranger, and it might be better to lie low for the time being. I could talk to Elaine and my brother, Hank, about it later.

An uneasy silence fell, so I took the list from my purse and slid it across to her. She went about collecting the items and putting them in a box. As she handed me change, a man wearing black jeans and a grimy tee shirt came in. He carried a shotgun, but as long as he kept it pointed at the floor, I thought we'd be all right. Missy slid behind me, peeking out, suddenly afraid.

"Give me a box of them birdshot shells," he demanded, "and another six-pack." He slapped several bills on the counter and turned to study me with bloodshot eyes.

"You must be the little lady from Orlando we been expecting," he drawled. "The one that bought the old place out at Living Spring. "This your girl?" I shuddered when he reached around me with bony fingers to scramble Missy's curls.

"Please don't," I said, shoving his arm aside with my elbow.

"Hey, Raker." Two equally disreputable-looking men swaggered in to join their friend. I stood motionless, hoping against hope they would let us take our purchases and leave without giving us any more unwelcome attention.

"She's the one—city gal; might need some showing around." The man puffed out his chest.

"All right!" they shouted, slapping into high-fives as if congratulating each other for some great accomplishment. I wasn't sure what they were celebrating, but I realized their delight ultimately meant no good for us. The one called Raker grabbed my wrist, and I drew back, giving him the most intimidating stare I could muster.

"Let go of me this instant," I said.

"Now that ain't a friendly way to treat your new neighbor." He held on. I tried to pull away, but the sound of rapidly approaching footsteps caught my attention. I looked up and my heart stopped. It was Richard Luskin, the father of my child! Where did he come from? I'd loved him so—once. Then I'd hated him. Now I didn't know; he looked good standing there in dress shorts and a crisp button-down shirt.

"Let go of her." The timbre in Richard's deep voice and the unmistakable authority in his tone made me melt. Raker's sneer left him and he released me.

"Richard," I said, keeping my voice as low and detached as possible. His white shirt, unbuttoned at the throat, gleamed in the soft light, and he moved with the ease of an athlete. That remembered smile…the faint drift of after-shave…I was lightheaded and dizzy with suppressed emotions. My legs began to tremble, and I braced myself against the counter…but I mustn't let him know how he was affecting me.

"Thank you," I said, now letting my voice become cold enough to freeze oranges on the trees. Not only was I unprepared to meet my former love, but I resented the other men staring as if we were players on a stage.

What were they looking at? Two people, once in love, who stood examining each other, and letting the years roll away, lonely years of confusion and guilt; for me, anyway. I recalled that when I first knew him, a courtly manner had made him the most sought-after tennis-pro in club history by the girls. The Harvard- and Princeton-bound young men, however, had sneered at his slicked-back ponytail and snubbed him. As for me, a look or a word had the power to keep me ricocheting between delight and despair.

My fingertips itched to touch that half-moon scar high on his cheekbone, but I couldn't afford any sign of vulnerability. He'd taken advantage of me once; what was to stop him from doing it again, especially if I didn't have the strength to resist him?

I'd known all along this country area held his original home, so why should I be surprised at seeing him here? Maybe it wasn't my brother and his wife who had brought me out of seclusion, but the thought of running into Richard. Subconsciously, I might have longed to see him, but in reality, I was far from ready. I straightened my shoulders, holding my body stiff and unyielding.

"It's been a long time," he said. "I missed you, babe." The amusement in his eyes told me he wasn't fooled for a minute.

"It was Fort Lauderdale." I started to babble helplessly, heading straight into the conflict between us. The last time I saw him was when I told him I was pregnant and he walked out of my life.

"Are you glad to see me, babe?" He stepped closer, proud and cocky. I stood my ground.

"I...don't know." My heart pounded with an almost audible thump. Glad, yes, but the gladness had an edge of defensiveness of not wanting to be hurt again. Missy's hand crept into my damp palm as she craned her neck to stare up at her father. At six-foot-four, he must have looked like a giant to her.

"Is this the kid?" He nodded toward our child.

"Yes--no thanks to you." Memory brought a knife thrust to my heart that sharpened into anger.

"What do you mean, 'no thanks' to me? You never would have had her without me, now would you?" His perfect white teeth gleamed in a self-satisfied grin.

I shot an embarrassed look at the storekeeper and the men who stood listening intently.

"Ah, you've got to admit, sweetheart, we had some good times." Richard's voice sounded low, intimate, just for me. The only problem was, he played to an audience that could hear him perfectly well.

By now, Missy had concluded a thorough inspection of the man who stood talking with her mother. She reached up to me.

"Pick me up," she demanded. I did as she said and she settled herself on my hip. "Is this my daddy?" she asked, looking deeply into my eyes.

"Yes, honey, he's your daddy. You've seen his picture, haven't you?" My hands trembled as I slid the drooping strap of her yellow sun-suit back onto her shoulder. I regretted that I had not prepared her to meet her father.

He chucked her under the chin, and she beamed with joy, but I didn't want to make it too easy for him. He tilted his head and ran his eyes up and down my body.

"Having a baby didn't hurt your figure any," Richard said. He perfectly understood the annoyed look I shot him, but his face remained alight with mischief.

"What's this, anyhow?" I stiffened when he reached out, but he was only going for the end of my French braid, which lay forward over my shoulder. "Does anybody still call you 'carrot top'?"

"My hair is auburn!" I bit my lip until it hurt. Once again, he'd taunted me into an outburst.

"Why don't you wear it loose? You know I like long hair on my women," he said.

"I'm not one of your women." I jerked my head to remove the braid from his fingers. "Why should I care what you think?"

"What did you say your name was, kid?" He spoke to her, now ignoring me.

"Melissa Suzanne," said Missy, showing four fingers, ahead of the obvious next question.

"You're an old lady of four, huh?" He smiled. "How about going for a hamburger?"

"And ice cream?" she bargained. Her tongue came out and ran around her lips.

"How about it, babe?" he asked me.

"Well…" I fingered the collar of my wrinkled plaid shirt. A girl prefers looking her best when she collides with the past. "I planned to get started sorting through the house in the morning. It's going to be a big job."

"We'll be done by morning," he said, teasing as he once had. "What on earth possessed you to buy that old rundown place, anyway? Isn't it full of junk? And I thought you hated the woods."

I supposed everyone in the community knew my business by now. Elaine warned me it would be so. Missy started humming the little tune that meant she needed the ladies' room, so we left Richard standing there and hurried toward the rear of the store where the restroom sign hung. I felt his eyes on my hips as I walked away. Outside, the rhythmic sound of cicadas rasped on, and the forlorn notes of a night bird reached us from deep in the woods. I shivered with apprehension.

The bathroom was clean, thank goodness. I opened the stall door for Missy, then went back to the sink and balanced my purse on its edge. When I dug around for a tube of lipstick, I found the cinnamon-colored one and I removed its cap.

Squinting into the tarnished mirror on the wall, I smoothed it over the lips that Richard had once found so kissable. My reflection sent back a message of heartfelt, never-quite-fulfilled yearnings from years of never fitting in. Missy needs him, I thought. He's her father; her flesh and blood. I do want a husband, more children, and a real home. I wonder if anybody, except Richard, would want us, but how can I believe he will ever change?

Suddenly, from the past, came Dr. Louise's voice. "Jean, you must develop some discernment about who to trust."

Ignoring the thought, I capped the lipstick and dropped it back into my purse, then loosened my hair and ran a pick through the molded waves that sprang out of control. I tried to smooth the unruly mass, but soon gave up. Richard would probably like it anyhow. Missy wanted to play in the water, but I washed her hands and face, took a deep breath, and marched forth.

CHAPTER 2

With his sneaker propped against a cold pot-bellied stove, Richard sat balancing on a captain's chair with his fingers linked behind his head. According to my study of body language, he felt superior to the situation and everyone in it.

"The old lady will hold your milk and stuff until we get back." He tipped forward to let the chair's front legs clunk to the floor. "Come on; we've got a lot of catching up to do."

He rolled his eyes to show how much patience I required and, as my old habit dictated, I doled out a tiny smile in return. Richard was often in a hurry from sheer exuberance and greed for living, but his impatience usually held an edge of anger that made me feel rushed and frustrated.

I maneuvered Missy's safety-seat, with her and her doll, into the back of his small red convertible, and soon we pulled out onto the highway.

"Are we going to get ice cream, Daddy?" Missy calling him "Daddy" was her way of getting used to a new, exciting idea. He didn't answer.

"Do you like the wheels?" he asked. "The car belongs to the boss, but I plan to buy one like it when I get rich." We sped through intermittent shadows as the setting sun flashed between the pines on either side of the road.

"Hank says the highway patrol is strict around here," I warned.

"Good ole Hank," he said derisively. "Is he the one who talked you into buying an old place way out here?" Richard did not lighten his foot on the gas pedal. "I thought you were a city gal."

"I'm determined to get used to country life." Richard didn't say anything, so I went on, explaining that I wanted to start a new life, that I had always wished I could renovate an old house, that we'd be close to Hank and Elaine, who had started a conservation and education effort close by.

My babbling reminded me of our short liaison when I spent half the time trying to make him understand me, and the rest of the time ignoring his criticism. I went on. "At Casa Del Sol, our housekeeper did all the work and took care of Missy as much as I'd let her, so I didn't have anything to do. I didn't want to spend all my time hanging around the club or playing bridge, so I thought I'd try fulfilling a life-long dream by renovating and decorating an already existing dwelling."

"Whatever happened to the old gal, anyway?" he asked.

"You mean Mrs. McGregor?" I said. "She's keeping house and cooking for Hank and Elaine at Sacred Spring. They're running a business and they're expecting, so they need help."

"You know we got snakes, gators, and lizards around here and a lot of them." He took his eyes off the road and looked over at me. "Aren't you the girl who was so terrified of snakes you couldn't even stand to look at pictures of them?" he teased. When he switched his gaze back to the road, I saw that he was still as handsome in profile as in full-face. His nose was proud and strong, his chin square with resolution.

"Yes, that's me," I confessed. "I do hate the country." One of the things Dr. Louise taught me was to tell the truth about myself and my feelings, even when talking to someone who was likely to ridicule me.

"Do you have any idea how noisy it is at night? There's screeching, peeping, honking—none of it human. Elaine's been teaching me about the birds, the bugs, and the animals. It's easing my fears—a bit. If I can just get used to all these sounds…"

"Did you miss me?" He put his hand on my knee, and the warmth instantly woke frozen places all over my body. Since he had left, I'd been half-dead and hadn't known it.

"What do *you* think?" I spoke sharply, hoping to make him leave me alone, but then I said, "You know how I felt about you." He inclined his head, and I saw he was really listening, so I continued. "Some of my friends thought a child out of wedlock was cool, but others and their parents shunned me."

"You wouldn't have gotten mixed up with me if your folks hadn't died, would you?" Richard glanced at me, and then back at the road. He seemed perfectly sure of himself, as if he'd never been away, as if I still belonged to him.

"By the way," I said, shaking my head, "where have you been these past four years?"

While seconds grew into minutes, I remembered Richard's policy of not answering questions, not wanting people to know his business. Through the windshield, I saw fast-moving clouds scrub the blue out of the sky and felt again the grief of my parents' death. I looked into the back seat to see Missy resting her chin on Raggedy Ann's red yarn hair and gazing dreamily at the back of Richard's head.

"Did you get through all the red tape about your inheritance?" he asked.

"We had to pay a lot of estate tax, but we finally got it straightened out. I was in a bad way emotionally then. I wonder how you ever put up with me."

"Hey, my pleasure, babe." He laughed.

I wasn't fond of his choice of words. Being with him had been almost pleasurable; but because Mother and Dad had taught me that going to the marriage bed a virgin was a worthy goal, and I had failed, shame stalked me every time I thought about him. He had been an obsession. I hoped I had learned my lesson, but I feared, now that I'd seen him again, I had not.

Richard wheeled into a parking space under a sign that read: ORANGE BLOSSOM PALACE: ALL NIGHT TRUCK STOP.

The bell on the door jangled as we walked in, and two burly truck drivers at the counter looked up. The aroma of frying hamburgers made me salivate. Missy had eaten breakfast and then a peanut butter and jelly sandwich for lunch, but I'd been too upset to eat. The diner's air-conditioner hummed valiantly.

Patsy Cline sang "Crazy" from a jukebox that had flashing colored lights. Its melody filled me with nostalgia for the days when Richard and I first met and all had seemed so right between us.

He leaned over to say softly, "Are you still crazy about me, babe? You can't imagine how much I missed you." My insides swooned with longing. He slipped his arm around my waist to direct me to a booth, and I leaned into him, dragging Missy along by the hand. We slid in close to a plate-glass window that looked out onto the parking lot where several eighteen-wheeled, hunchbacked dinosaurs rested in the growing dark.

A green pick-up with a trailered boat pulled in next to one of the behemoths, and a tall, slender man got out. I watched him walk around to the passenger side and open the door to release a big, black Labrador retriever with floppy ears. The man, with his dark curly hair and short, neat beard, looked familiar.

Just then, a short, partridge-plump waitress bounced over. "Hi, I'm Bess. What a beautiful little girl you've got there." She plucked a pencil from a rooster tail of frizzy gray hair. "Now, what can I get you folks?" Before we could reply, the tall man strode in and spun her around, enfolding her in a hug.

"Hi, Mom." His uniform was elegant with knife-sharp creases. The insignia read, "Florida Department of Fish and Wildlife," and the name badge identified him as "Thaddeus Nicolaides."

"Hi, Thaddeus." The waitress beamed.

"Call me 'Nick,' okay, Mom?" He shot me a glance.

"Thaddeus Adonis Nicolaides, that's the *monica* we gave you when you was born and there's no way you can slide out from under it." She wiggled all over like a joyful puppy. What must it be like to have a grown son? Maybe someday I would know.

"Hello, Jean," said Nick. "Remember me? I see you've already met my mother, Bess."

"Why, yes. You're Elaine's cousin, aren't you? We met at Elaine and Hank's wedding." I politely introduced Richard. Nick looked straight at him without smiling and reached over the table to shake

hands. Although the gesture might have seemed friendly, they glared at each other like wrestlers going into a match.

"This is my kid," Richard said with a grim nod at Missy. Suddenly back in the slough of shame where I had already spent so much time, I chewed on the soft flesh inside my lower lip in consternation.

"Yes! The sweet flower girl at Hank and Elaine's wedding." Nick took the tiny hand extended in imitation of her father, and his good-natured smile returned. "Who's that you've got with you?"

"This is Raggedy Ann," said Missy, holding her doll up to be admired.

"Hello, Raggedy Ann." Nick touched the doll hand Missy thrust at him. "Well, I'll see you around," he said before walking away. "I'm going to wash up." In a minute, he was back and sitting down at the counter with a man in another kind of uniform. He punched him playfully. "Hey, buddy did you catch any criminals today?"

"Ice cream." Missy's loud demand reclaimed my attention.

"What kind you want, sweetie?" Bess said. "We got vanilla, chocolate, and *pistachimo*." Bess smiled at Missy while the child screwed her face in concentration.

"Don't you mean 'pistachio'?" I said, puzzled.

"Yes, dear, pistachimo, that's what I said." Bess clearly was having a good time. "Say, you're going to be an auntie soon, aren't you? How do you think you'll like that? We can be aunts together, because I'll be the great aunt. Elaine's my niece, you know."

"Oh, of course, but I didn't see you at the wedding." I hoped I was right; it would be embarrassing if she had attended and I didn't remember.

"My daughter was sick over in Oviedo, and I had to look after her and the kids." She smiled, obviously loving to be needed.

At a stern, let's-get-on-with-it look from Richard I told her, "I'd like a diet cola, and two burgers, one for Missy and one for me. Are you having one, Richard?"

"Diet? What for?" Bess asked. "You're already too skinny, and besides diet stuff is full of car-mikals."

Never before had a waitress argued with my order. She wasn't fazed by my open-mouthed astonishment, but went right on. "Why don't you drink some real cola and put some meat on your bones, honey?"

"Just bring four hamburgers!" Richard snapped. Bess looked hurt, but turned and walked away without another word. Richard reached across the table for my hands. "I've missed you."

"You found us that one time, though, didn't you? Where have you been since then?" I lowered my eyes, hoping to be able to question him without starting a fight. I needed courage, so I asked the Lord for it.

"I've been in the joint," he muttered.

"The joint?" I looked fully at him then, and knew I was frowning. "You mean you've been in prison? Richard! What for?"

"Did a deuce. That's not so much," he answered.

"What does that mean?" I asked, annoyed with his prison lingo. I pulled my hands away. "I've never known anyone before who was in prison."

"I'm rehabilitated—a changed man. You gotta let it go." Richard's dark gaze smoldered into mine, but I was too shaken to answer or to give him the reassurance he was always looking for.

"Babe?" his voice appealed.

"What did you go to prison for?" Anger clipped each word to make it clear to him that I was not going to accept his constant evasions of the truth.

"For nothing. I swear to God." He held up his hand, palm showing in a vow-taking gesture and more alarm bells jangled.

Dr. Louise had taught me, as part of my emotional self-defense, to watch a speaker's eyebrows. Richard's right one was twitching like a dying fly. Dr. Louise also taught me that when someone said *I swear to God* or *Trust me,* it usually meant they were in the habit of lying. It all seemed backwards, somehow, but I squared my shoulders and vowed silently to use Dr. Louise's wise sayings as a shield when dealing with Richard Luskin.

"They don't put people in prison for no reason," I said. "Why don't you just tell me?"

"Ah, they found a smidgen of coke in the old Cessna." He

measured an inch in the air with thumb and forefinger, to him obviously an insignificant amount.

"How did it get there?" I asked.

"I got enemies," he said, scowling.

"But, Richard, drugs?" I couldn't help shaking my head, even knowing it would probably send him into a rage.

"I know." He shrugged. "But I wasn't using; just increasing my portfolio." He snorted as he laughed, obviously enjoying his own sense of humor.

Bess returned with a round, cork-lined tray holding a bottle of beer, a tall glass, a diet soda, and a cone with two scoops of green ice cream. "Your burgers will be here in a jiffy," she said as she rushed off again.

"You wanted to know, so now you know. At least I'm honest." He angled his glass and tipped the bottle slowly so that the liquid flowed without foaming.

Missy licked her ice cream, humming with enjoyment. I knew a better mother would give her daughter real food before letting her eat dessert, but I wasn't in control of my mothering at the moment. I grabbed a handful of napkins to stanch the rivulets running down her arm and dripping off her elbow onto the table.

"She's making a mess." Richard reared back against the seat as if to say keep her away from me, and irritation clenched my jaws. I had a feeling he'd never be much of a dad. Why didn't I let him go—again? Then I rationalized, he's not accustomed to kids. He might need a little help at first.

"Richard, will you please ask for a dish?" I said. "It's melting too fast."

"Yes, ma'am!" he said, saluting. He caught the waitresses' eye as she came away from the booth behind me. After he ordered the needed china, he reached for my hand. "You're not going to turn against me now, are you?" Such a hangdog face, how could anyone resist?

"Tell me about prison—was it really bad?" I was surprised at my own boldness and took it as a sign of growth.

"No, it was a big party all the time," he said with sarcasm. "Jean, if you'd ever been in the slammer, you wouldn't ask such a dumb question. But I will tell you this: *you* wouldn't last five minutes." He sighted me over his index finger and clicked an imaginary trigger.

"It has never been my ambition to survive in prison." I looked him in the eye, feeling unusually self-confident.

"Come on, let's get out of here," he said suddenly. He plucked Missy from her seat and slung her under his arm. She giggled and dropped her cone on the floor, then began wailing for it.

"But...?" I was embarrassed now and wished I hadn't challenged him. Knowing from experience that he would sweep past the cash register on the way out. I hurried to pull a twenty from my wallet and throw it on the table to pay the bill. I would return another time to make sure that was enough. I was embarrassed, but I gave Nick a glance as I passed, and he lifted his mug in a silent, comforting salute.

As we walked out, I thought hungrily of the hamburgers that would soon be delivered to our table. Mrs. McGregor had taught us to abhor the wasting of food, so I hoped the waitress would give them to Nick and his friend. Those two looked as if they could eat any number of hamburgers.

Richard set a snuffling Missy on the hood of his car while he got out his key. I picked her up, feeling guilty about her hunger and disappointment. I thought that perhaps she was frightened as well. I did not think of myself as a perfect mother, but I tried not to upset her unnecessarily.

"Put her in back and let's go." I smoothed tendrils of hair around the tiny ears while he tapped his fingers on top of the car. She began sucking her thumb and, for once, I let her.

We drove to the general store to get the car and pick up the milk, eggs, and butter. Soon, Richard would go and Missy and I could get to the house, unpack fresh sheets, make up a bed, and eat a bowl of cereal. A night's rest would surely restore our peace.

By the time we drew up in front of the three-story house, Missy was into one of her deep sleeps where nothing could wake her. Still, I didn't want to take a chance by getting her out of the car seat, so Richard followed me to Living Spring with her in his car because once you woke her, she wouldn't easily go back to sleep.

While I unloaded the groceries, he carried my still-snoozing daughter, in her seat, upstairs to a clean bedroom. After I had put some of the groceries on the counter and some in the refrigerator, I went up to wash her hands and face and saw Richard perched on the end of the bed as if he belonged there.

A tremor of fear mixed with excitement warned me I should have asked him to come right back down. It might not have done any good because he never liked taking orders, but I would have felt a lot safer with him in the kitchen than in a bedroom.

Missy whimpered, "Raggedy Ann" in her sleep, so I gave Richard a pleading look to check the car. From the moment he left, I was able to breathe without the constriction in my chest.

"I love you," I whispered to Missy, "more than life itself." I moved her in her seat to the overstuffed chair, put clean sheets on the bed, then carefully unbuckled the seat and moved her to the bed.

Richard was waiting at the foot of the stairs. "No doll." He shrugged as if it were nothing to worry about.

"Do you want something to eat?" I steeled myself to stay cool.

"What's all the junk in the front room?" he asked, following me to the kitchen.

"Mostly antiques." I answered. "The place came as is. Annie, the lady who owned it before, is a friend of Elaine's. Her ancestors built it in the 1800s, but Annie's parents made part of it into an antique shop before World War II.

"I'm going to go through everything and auction off most of it before I start to renovate." I touched the brown framing around the kitchen doorway. "My plan is to make it as light and airy as possible. I hope the house will stand up to a make-over."

At the kitchen sink, Richard leaned in and tried to take me in his arms. I couldn't miss the desire in his eyes. I sidled away, talking fast.

"We could find termites in the beams or wood-rot. I might have to remove paneling, rip up carpets..."

"I'll be getting a new airplane," Richard said, cutting into my monologue. "And right now, I'm looking for a place to stay."

"I'll fix you a hot dog," I said. "And then, you'll have to go." I worked quickly, setting water on the stove to boil and opening a package of frankfurters. At home, Mrs. McGregor did all the cooking, but at least I knew how to boil water for hot dogs.

"I've got a job," Richard announced, seating himself where he could watch me from the table. "Raker says they need a gamekeeper-slash-tennis pro at my folks' old place. I'll feel weird being a hired hand instead of the boss's son, but if I get enough money, I can buy that airplane and make some real dough. Dad won't leave me anything unless I prove I can make it on my own."

"So you already have a place to stay?" He gave me a sheepish grin that said, you couldn't blame a guy for trying. It made me furious, so furious I blurted, "Hank said you've been in a lot of trouble."

"At least I don't run security checks on people. That's just plain snooping." As far as I knew, Hank was innocent of wrongdoing, but that was hard for Richard to grasp. I almost backed off, but I was compelled to find out about his life since I'd last seen him.

"Let me get this straight. You've been in prison, but the drugs weren't yours." I half wished he'd convince me he was a victim, not a criminal. It would certainly make me feel better about having chosen him when I had so desperately needed to be loved and comforted.

"Yeah, there were twenty-eight grams. Twenty-nine, and we would have gotten more than the deuce." He tapped his fingers on the table.

"Why were you hanging around drugs, anyhow?" I asked.

"Got any mustard?" Richard frowned at the hot dog I put in front of him.

"No, I forgot to buy any." I shrugged off his unspoken displeasure. Then sticking to the subject, I said, "You took me to Ft. Lauderdale because your uncle wanted you to become a pilot so you could give flying lessons." I hoped we could strive for a bit of truth in our new relationship…*if* we were going to have one.

"How could I know they were using the student planes to run stuff? You gotta admit it would have been a good cover if they hadn't got caught. Myself, I was just taking lessons." He bit into the soft bun and chewed. "The last time I landed, the place was crawling with blue shirts. They got a tip, and I got jail time."

"Why didn't you call me?" I said, wishing I was needed by someone besides Missy.

"Because they only let me make one call, and I didn't want to spend it on hearing a lecture. I figured the court-appointed lawyer would have some smarts, but he didn't." His teeth glinted in a grimace meant to resemble a smile. "I knew how mad you were because you thought it was me who got you pregnant."

"It was you!" Feeling the rage heating up, I almost shouted at him. "You didn't leave because I was pregnant; you left because I refused to have an abortion." How dare he accuse me of sleeping with someone else when he was the only boy I had ever loved? Eventually, I realized that losing my temper wasn't going to get us anywhere, and I took a couple of good, deep breaths.

"I didn't care if you did. I just wanted to get on with our lives. We could have too, if you hadn't been so stubborn. Didn't you find out that raising a kid took all your time and was a lot of trouble? I knew that in advance." He drank from the soda can I'd given him. "Ugh! If I'm going to be coming to see you, you'll have to stock up on some beer."

"You'll be glad to know it wasn't entirely your fault," I told him, trying now to soothe the troubled waters. "My counselor said I needed help with the original grief from when my parents died in the plane crash, and that I made a mistake when I latched onto you because you were in no shape to do me any good. I was sad that you didn't believe she was yours. It mattered to me whether I slept around or not, mattered a lot. The worst disappointment was when I knew you would want her destroyed before she even had a chance to live."

"So? I never thought any of it was my fault," Richard said with a sneer. "Dumb broads are always getting themselves into that kind of trouble." He quickly pressed his thumb against his lips as if he'd said more than he meant to.

"I was in a program for people in unhealthy relationships," I continued. Suddenly I became aware of a squeezed feeling in my ankles. I looked down and saw them wrapped around the legs of my chair. I put my feet under the table, but Richard's legs took up all the space, so I slipped them under my chair again.

"I don't know what all the fuss is about." He looked up at the ceiling. "You didn't do anything wrong except want to be with me. Women are just that way." After a pause, he continued, "I mean like my mom and my aunts. Dad says they spoiled me into thinking I could have my way with all women."

"Tell me about prison," I asked softly, having already heard about his success with women—from him.

"They made us get up at 4:00 A. M., unload the food truck, cook breakfast for all the inmates, wash tons of steel trays, mop the kitchen and mess hall, and start on the midday meal. After lunch, we washed all those trays again, went out for yard time, then went back to peel potatoes and serve supper.

"Other guys worked in the laundry, and some made license plates. I tried that. The good ones made a thousand a shift, press, coat, dry, polish, pack. I was so bored with the whole set up that I wanted to claw my way out of there with my bare hands. I tell you, the boredom is the pits. I'd kill before I'd go back."

"What about the fighting and all that?" I took a sip of water.

"Yeah." His expression told me my naiveté amused him. "You mean, did I see a guy knifed in the shower, and blood spurting all over the place? I did; he deserved it. Nobody messed with me about the girly thing, though. I was too tough for that." He played with my fingers as he once had. I wondered if that wasn't part of his technique.

"Look, babe," he said, "I need you to help me." I leaned forward. "I went to Bible study classes, and got religion. You know all about that stuff and you can teach me." He hesitated, searching my face for clues, and then he nodded eagerly. "Okay?"

"Well, sure," I said, astonished out of my pique. "I never dreamed I'd hear anything like that from you. Why didn't you say so sooner? I'd love to share with you. This is great!" I jumped up and almost sat down in his lap, but before I could fall into his arms, I saw car lights flicker across the ceiling.

That made me pause. I realized I was putting myself into his hands, again, a bit too readily, too quickly. Glad for a reprieve, I ran to the window over the sink, and looked out to see Nick's truck pull up. Peace flooded over me as I hurried to the door.

"Hi," I said too heartily. "Come on in."

"Your little girl left this." He handed me Raggedy Ann.

"Thanks!" I clasped her to my chest. "Missy will be glad to see her."

"I hope I'm not bothering you," he said. "I had to come out this way anyhow."

"Not at all." I gripped his arm with fingers of steel and pulled him through the back porch and into the kitchen.

"Only for a minute," he said, coming along. I wondered what Richard would think when he saw him.

"I saw the truck lights coming through the woods. Don't you ever worry about getting stuck on that sandy road?"

"It's a four-wheel, off-road vehicle. I get stuck sometimes, not here, but it's easy to get unstuck with the winch. "

"Richard, here's Nick again," I announced as we entered the room. But no one was there. Outside, an engine purred to life. He hadn't even waited to say goodbye. But I had something good to think about him now. He wanted to learn about God. How wonderful.

"Took off, huh?" Looking at home in the big kitchen, Nick moved casually to the counter and started unpacking the groceries I had forgotten. He put the dry packages in the cupboards and the cooler items in the ancient refrigerator. "Haven't you got anything to drink except diet soda?"

"That's all." I cleared Richard's plate from the table then leaned over the sink and opened the window. November wafted in, touching my face with night smells of spicy, verdant growth and welcome coolness.

Nick turned his chair with the back toward the table and straddled it, then popped open a can of soda. I couldn't help noticing how his somewhat prominent Adam's apple bobbed as he drank it down. "Whew, I hate this stuff." He tossed the empty can across the room where it rattled into the coalscuttle next to the range.

"Hey, that was expert." I said, laughing. "Are you a basketball player?"

"Used to be. Good thing it didn't go on the floor. That's no way to impress a lady."

With Richard's exit, the heaviness had lifted, and I was beginning to enjoy myself. It didn't matter what I said; Nick just wanted company. The antique ceiling lamp, converted from gas to electricity, cast a soft glow over his face.

"You and I are cousins-in-law," I said. Because I felt attracted to him, but didn't want to complicate things, I drew a line between us. "That means we can be good friends."

"I'd hardly call us relatives," he said. His eyes twinkled as he looked deeply into mine.

"Your cousin is my brother's wife. That's close enough," I insisted.

"But you and I are not related to each other," he insisted as he got up and went to the refrigerator for another soda.

"Do you want a hot dog?" I got him one.

"I never pass them up. Got anything sweet? You ought to taste Mom's baklava. She learned to bake it for dad because he was Greek. It's so rich with honey and *pistachimos* you can only eat a small slice at a time." He grinned and I knew he was thinking about his mother.

"How about animal crackers?" I asked, knowing Missy had selected them at the general store. I opened the box and held it out to him.

Nick was so down to earth that I'd guessed he'd relish kid food. In the days ahead, however, I'd have to make him understand that we were shirttail relatives--and friends--and could never be more.

"I don't want to eat your little girl's cookies," he answered, then at my disappointed expression, he said, "But sure, I like them almost as much as Mom's baking." He reached into the box and brought out a partial cookie. "It doesn't have a trunk," he said, sticking out his lower lip in a surprisingly accurate mime of a pouting four-year-old.

"Have this zebra, too." I laid another one in front of him, pretending to placate.

"What kind of mother would give away her kid's animal crackers, anyhow," he said, and popped it into his mouth.

"One who knows her child is perfectly capable of getting more." I laughed, delighted with his playfulness.

"Delicious!" He sighed, closing his eyes. "It's almost as good as Mom's chocolate cake. She puts mayonnaise in it. Do you like mayonnaise?"

"Mayo is okay, but chocolate—well, I like chocolate any way I can get it, especially bittersweet." I smiled as I thought about the differences between him and Richard.

CHAPTER 4

"**W**hy did your friend run off?" Nick stood so he could reach into his pants pocket for a lump of silver-gray wood. From his shirt came a small case. He opened it and carefully chose a tool, then began to pare the wood, turning it this way and that.

"Who knows?" I shrugged. "Richard is strange sometimes. How do you do that?" I asked, watching his fingers move gracefully over the carving.

"My hands seem to know the shape of things." He held it up and looked at it with a puzzled frown. His hands weren't huge like Richard's, but slender with the long straight fingers of a surgeon or a musician. "But I use photos to check the details." Thin shavings drifted to the floor, making me wonder if he usually had someone to clean up after him.

"You enjoy the woods, don't you?" I asked.

"Sure do." He nodded. "You haven't lived until you've gone out before dawn and set up blind to take pictures. It's like watching the world wake up. Birds pour out songs; the sky turns from purple to rose. And, ah, the pure fragrance of the outdoor air." The laugh lines around his eyes deepened as he smiled to himself.

"What do you photograph?" I was anxious to learn more from an experienced woodsman like Nick. I found sitting here talking to him intriguing and comforting, like coming home after a long journey.

"Funny thing is, birds, deer, raccoon, whatever you're after, they know you're there, but as long as you're a gentleman and keep still, you can take all the pictures you want. I'd stay later, but the blind gets suffocating as the day progresses." He blew dust off the carving and continued working. "Would you like to go with me sometime?" he asked, head down pretending, I thought, that it didn't matter whether I went or not.

"Yes, I'd like to; maybe I could get someone to watch Missy." It sounded exciting.

"Are you planning to stay around here?" he asked.

"I don't know yet. I'm going to renovate the house and after that, it depends." I twisted the tablecloth, nervous about not having any concrete plans for going on after the house was finished.

"If you need help with carpentry, child care, cooking ..." he asked.

"You do all that?" I said.

His booming laugh filled the room. "No, I'm just a carpenter. Mom's a great housekeeper, though, and she's looking for another job. She hates that restaurant. Do you cook?"

Childcare took a great deal of time, as did laundry and cleaning. I'd been wondering how I'd find time to do all that, go through the antiques, keep track of the business, and redecorate this great rummage of a house.

"Not much." I shook my head. "But I'm good at investments." I was embarrassed to admit my lack of practical skills to a man who, if he could not do it all, was at least familiar with what it took to do it all.

"What do you feed that poor little girl?" I was surprised when he skipped over my only real talent. Most people wanted to discuss money, ad infinitum, ad nauseam, but he was a different sort altogether.

"We've been getting by on hot dogs, cereal, and canned soup since Mrs. McGregor left…. Mrs. McGregor," I echoed, nostalgically. "I didn't like giving her up, but with your and Elaine's granddad still a semi-invalid, Annie appreciates her help. Honestly, with their environmental school, consulting firm, and camp for inner-city kids where will they get time to be parents? How is Ira, anyway?" I asked.

"He's doing all right, but Annie hardly gives him a chance to do anything for himself," Nick said, and then he abruptly changed the subject. "How do you like being on your own?"

"I don't know yet. I think country living could terrify me." I smoothed the tablecloth. Outside, I heard a dog bark. "What's that?"

"It's Zorba," Nick said. "Could he come in, do you think?" He put down the carving and jumped up eagerly. "He gets lonesome," he added when I hesitated.

"I'm not used to having dogs inside." I stalled him, not sure what would happen next.

"He's housebroken, and he won't bother anything."

"I guess ..." I said, and he was gone. I thought about the dog getting lonesome. I knew that feeling. The screen door banged, and the big, black Labrador retriever sat at my feet and put his paw on my knee.

"Talk to him," Nick commanded. "He won't hurt you. He's a pussycat."

"But he's growling." I folded my arms over my chest.

"That's not growling; it's his happy groan. Say, 'Hi, Zorba'. Dogs are like kids--they like to hear their names." Nick watched fondly while I patted the animal's head with the tips of my fingers.

Zorba wagged his tail so fast I was afraid if it gave me a whack, it might break my leg. I put my hand back in my lap, but he pushed at it with his muzzle, communicating as clearly as if he were using words. He was shiny and clean and I wondered if he'd recently had a bath. Nick obviously took good care of him.

"He is beautiful and he knows how to communicate," I conceded.

"Okay, buddy, go lie down now." The animal obeyed reluctantly, stretching himself across the doorway, head up, eyes alert in case we needed him.

"I think I can help with both your problems," Nick said.

"What do you have in mind?" I felt cozy and cared for.

"Mom is good with kids—she's got us four and eight grandkids— nine, soon.

"And the cooking, and other jobs?" I tilted my head.

"I'll leave Zorba here with you; there's nothing to be afraid of, but having him would make you feel safer. He's a fine watchdog and gentle with children. Aren't you, boy?" Nick spoke across the room and the dog's tail thumped the floor.

"You'd give me your mom *and* your dog?" I asked, happy with anticipation.

"I'd have to pick up the dog every morning for work. He's my partner. I don't think I could get along without him. The rest of the time, he's yours." Nick fell silent, concentrating on the carving. "Sometimes I have to work at night."

"But would Zorba stay without you?" I looked at the big dog and imagined him wanting to go wherever his master went.

"Here's the situation. Mom and I live in an apartment over the truck stop. We get a discount on the rent because my being there provides security. When we're home, he lies around with his nose on his paws, looking bored and depressed. He'd enjoy a little girl to look after and you can let him patrol the perimeters of your place.

"He won't run off or get into trouble. Think it over. It's not a package deal. You want Mom, you get Mom; you want Zorba, you get Zorba, and of course, you don't have to hire me, it's just that I'm here if you want to. Think about it." His hand once again gripped the handle of the curved knife as the little creature resumed its metamorphosis.

"What are you making, anyway?" I asked.

"A manatee and her offspring," he answered. "You can't quite see them yet." He handed the piece to me, and its smoothness caressed my palm. It already resembled a living, breathing animal with its own personality. He was quite an artist.

"In the winter, the manatees swim up into the spring from the St. Johns River in order to stay warm," he said.

"I've seen pictures, but I don't know much about them." I studied the model in my hand.

"They can weigh up to two thousand pounds--as much as a Brahma bull." He took the unfinished carving back and turned it. "Does it remind you of a walrus?" He tapped the short, fat proboscis.

"In other words, you cross a walrus and a Brahma bull and you get a manatee, right?" I reached out to stroke the smooth wood he held in his cupped hand. "I hear they are in danger of becoming extinct."

"Yes," he said. "They do take an awful beating in the wild. They graze on water plants such as hyacinth, which is good because those invasive plants can clog a body of water in no time; but that makes manatees feed in the waterways where boaters go and those guys don't always slow down through there. That's when the manatees get sliced with boat propellers. They can be killed or scarred for life. Almost every manatee I've ever seen bears those wounds.

"If they don't get to warm water in the winter, they can die of hypothermia, or they can become entangled in monofilament fishing line, which causes infections and loss of flippers." He touched the carving with his finger. "See that tiny knob up there under her flipper? That's where junior gets his grub."

"How can they breathe?" He obviously loved talking about these strange animals and I loved hearing it.

"Immediately after birth, the mother swims under him and lifts him to the surface to breathe. She keeps on until he learns to do it for himself, but if too many boats or too much noise disturbs the training period, he'll drown."

"That is truly awful, poor little things." I took the emerging creature from his hand again. "Do you use a lot of different kinds of wood?" I asked, absorbing the details.

"Yes, I have a whole collection—pine, hickory, and oak—for different birds and animals. You have to pick it up off the ground after it's seasoned, but before it rots or gets riddled by termites holes. I'm on the lookout for it all the time."

"Do you sell your work?" I asked.

"I need to; they would crowd me out of the apartment." His eyes widened in mock surprise. It was obvious he loved the animals in his menagerie so much that he hated the thought of parting with them.

"Granddad Ira started teaching me when I was about six." He gave a short laugh, but sobered immediately. "What do you think about my ideas?" He was getting back to the question under discussion. "I'd like to know Zorba was looking after you and your daughter." He got up, took the broom and dustpan from beside the back door, and while he waited for my answer, swept up the shavings and threw them into the coal bucket.

"I could use your mother's help, and I'd like her to move in, if she would. You're sure leaving Zorba off and picking him up wouldn't be too much trouble? I think I'd sleep better, knowing he was on night duty."

"No trouble at all." He sighed and relaxed into the chair. He handed me the finished carving. "Do me a favor and take care of this."

CHAPTER 5

$\mathcal{I}$ was grateful that so far, Nick had managed to restrain his natural curiosity, but it eventually got the better of him.

"What about your friend—why did he leave, or don't you want to tell me?" His light-filled eyes fascinated me.

"Maybe he's shy?" I said, taking note of how whole, how sane, how trustworthy Nick seemed.

"Yeah, right!" He didn't believe me. Why should he? I wasn't telling the truth.

"I can't imagine the two of you getting along, and the less I say to either of you about the other, the better off we'll all be," I said.

"Okay, we won't talk about him." Nick stretched out his legs and crossed his arms over his chest.

"You remembered that the flower girl at Hank and Elaine's wedding was Missy?" I said, taking off in another direction.

"Yes." Nick smiled. "She walked straight up the aisle to you, said, 'pick me up,' and when you did, she dumped her flower basket in a pile on the floor at your feet." We both laughed.

"You looked handsome in your tux." I said, watching fascinated as his cheeks took on a sunset flush. I couldn't recall seeing a man blush before.

"My monkey suit." He squeezed his throat with both hands, and I recalled the several times at the reception when he had run his finger around the inside of the collar, looking as if he'd like nothing better than to peel right out of that suit and jump in a river.

"You wanted to get back to your dog and your truck." He nodded in agreement.

"The best thing about the whole wedding..." he paused, "was you in that pink dress. You were the most beautiful thing I've ever seen. You took my breath away."

For a minute, I didn't know how to reply, and then I decided on a light touch to hide my elation at receiving the compliment. "Hank went overboard at the florist. That's why you couldn't breathe. By the way, the dress was peach."

"Pink—peach—what's the difference?" he asked. "You were beautiful, and no flowers could have done what you did to me. It was funny, because I actually had never been affected in just that way before." Comfortable in the roomy, old-fashioned kitchen, neither of us seemed able to stop smiling over nothing, over everything; we fell into a soft silence as the call of a chuck-will's-widow floated in the open window. The grandfather clock bonged ten times in the hallway.

"I think Elaine felt intimidated; she's not used to a church that big. It's nice, though. Have you gone there all your life?" he asked.

"They put me on the cradle roll when I was a week old. They would have done it the day I was born, but they had to wait for the lady in charge of the nursery to get back from vacation." I felt like talking all night until I remembered Nick's schedule. "What time do you have to go to work in the morning?"

"Early; I should go." He began to fidget in his chair, yet made no move to leave.

"I didn't mean that. I'm enjoying myself. Can you stay a little longer? It helps to have somebody here while I'm getting used to the idea of spending my first night in this jungle." He reached across the table for my hand, but I quickly put it in my lap where he couldn't touch it.

"Sorry, that's a habit from when my wife..." His voice cracked.

"You're married? I didn't see your wife at the wedding." My heart was in the pit of my stomach, and I didn't stop to question why.

"She died," he said, looking away from me.

"What happened?" Distress battled with relief. How could so kind a man have suffered such deep hurt? His hurt was obviously greater than any I had ever experienced.

"Car accident." He looked away, struggling to control his emotions. Finally, he spoke. "Our little girl was stillborn." I could barely hear as he lowered his head and clasped his hands between his open knees. "She would be about Missy's age now." The struggle to repress his grief vibrated in his voice.

I felt the hot sting of empathetic tears and searched wildly for something to say lest my anxiety embarrass him.

"Richard is Missy's father," I uttered impulsively. "When he left me, I thought I'd die, but the death of a wife and child must be so much more…"

"Final," he said.

"I shouldn't have fallen for Richard." I wanted to cover for the embarrassment I sensed in him. Now that I had started my story, I wanted Nick to know I wasn't promiscuous. "God has forgiven me," I said.

"But you haven't forgiven yourself." He downed the last of his cola and made another basket in the coal scuttle.

"I haven't?" I reared back in my chair, shocked by his perceptiveness.

"You're still carrying a big load of guilt," he said.

"No, I'm not!" I felt myself withdrawing from the conversation. "I'm going to make it right, that's all!" Twinges pinched at my temples, signaling the onset of a headache.

"How are you going to make it right?" He settled back, prepared to listen with all his being. It was rare to know someone who wanted to hear what I had to say. Vaguely ashamed that I had avoided listening to the end of his tale, I tried to set aside my defenses and pretensions, and converse honestly with him.

"I have a tentative plan to marry Richard when I finish the house. If it all works out, we'll make a home together here, and have more children. And you know what I'd really like to do?" I didn't wait for him to speak, but continued at his nod. "There's so much room here, I'd like to do something for families that need help. It's a dream of mine."

"What do you think Richard will say about all that?" he asked. "Listen, your plans sound fine — if you love him and if you think he can take good care of you and the children you plan on having. But if you don't love him and if he won't…"

I waited while he got up and turned on the small radio on top of the refrigerator. Its melancholy country song made my heart plummet.

"It's none of my business, of course," he continued. He stepped to the back door as Zorba scrambled out of his way. He drew in a long breath of fresh air, then went over to the sink, drank some water, washed the glass, and faced me again, resting against the edge of the counter. Whatever he'd been about to say, he apparently thought better of it.

"Thanks for the soda pop and your company. You've decided you want Mom and the dog, right?" Just before he disappeared through the back door he said, "Zorba, stay." And suddenly, except for the dog's tail hitting against the old linoleum, and the symphony of cicadas outside, the house fell silent.

The next morning in my upstairs bedroom, sunlight coming through the French windows lit the room as I struggled to get my legs out from under the heavy weight that was lying on them.

I remembered frogs peeping and crickets thrumming throughout the night as I wakened, listened for approaching cars, and slept again. The dog lifted his head and placidly watched me. I laid my head back down. The large room was cool and restful with its white walls and blue accents. Thanks to the popularity of "shabby chic," there would be little need for change.

A small tremor caused me to look at the other side of the bed and there was Missy smiling at me. I recalled staggering back to bed with her in my arms after hearing her cry in the night. What a crowd I had collected, I thought smiling to myself. I pushed at the dog with my feet and he slid to the floor, then I pulled Missy close and sang,

"Who is that sleeping in my bed, little girl with hair of red?"

"It's me!" she sang out. Looking at her mop of topsy-turvy curls, I wondered how I'd brush through without her "pitching a western," as my father used to call my own tantrums.

I picked up my watch from a stack of old books on the nightstand.

"We slept late, didn't we? Give me a bear hug, and we'll get some breakfast."

She crawled onto my chest where she lay small and warm. She growled and I answered in kind while squeezing her in my arms. Happy and refreshed in the white wrought iron bed with its gold trim and blue counterpane, I thanked God for all he had done for us.

"Someday we'll have a daddy here. You'll wake him, and we'll all be a happy together."

"Where's Daddy?" she asked, growing still.

"He went away for awhile, but now he's coming back." I knew it would be hard, but I was determined, as she grew, to answer her questions honestly. Later, she would understand, but without making the same mistakes I'd made.

I set Missy down and she pattered over the polished floor to the armchair where she clambered up and stuck out her legs, trying in vain to reach the matching hassock. Failing that, she curled on the cushion like a cat to wait. I took another satisfied look around as I donned shorts and a plaid shirt.

A lady's small oak desk stood in the corner. Its surface held a quill pen in an ivory holder and a cobalt inkstand that looked as if they had been partners for centuries. I glanced out the window and saw a vine-covered water tower. Elaine had told me about the history of the house and I knew the first occupants were progressive in many ways. They were the first in the area to have running water, and they changed over to electricity early on, harnessing power from the nearby spring.

"Let's get you into a fresh sun suit," I said.

"I want my pink tutu, please, Mommy." She jumped to the floor and started to pirouette. As I found only one clean tee shirt and pair of shorts, I indulged her. We would do laundry soon. As soon as Bess came, I'd get started sorting and organizing.

After breakfast, we went into the parlor to start work, and I propped the windows open with sticks that waited on the sill for that purpose. I'll install new windows, I thought. They have so many beautiful ones to choose from these days. The room had no curtains, but I decided to buy lace tiebacks or have them made to suit the spirit of the house.

Between two of the windows, a segment of wall jutted out about five feet, looking as if it was hiding something. I made a mental note to ask about it. Later on, we would remove the green shag carpet that covered the floor and put down new wood floors like the ones upstairs, if they weren't already there under the carpet.

Chairs, couches, and tables filled the middle of the room while boxes stood against the walls, waiting to be unpacked after many decades. It had been years since Annie actually sold anything here. Art quality pottery held dead plants and I vowed to learn about growing things so I could fill them with the life they deserved. I sat on the floor and began to unpack a crate of china.

"I want to help," Missy said, picking up a teacup with a paper-thin rim. "Need help?"

"No, sweetheart." I placed one hand under the cup and with the other took it gently. "Let's put that down; it's too old and fragile."

After a short time, I heard her humming and looked up to see her kneeling in front of an antique cradle filled with valuable period dolls. She held one that looked as if it represented a German sailor. With its stiff body, it was far from being a cuddly toy, but I sensed rarity and wanted to preserve it until we got an appraisal.

"Leave him alone, honey. We don't want anything to happen to him. Where's Raggedy Ann?"

"Sleeping." Missy lay her cheek against her hands to demonstrate.

I looked at the doll cradle. Sure enough, Raggedy Ann was sprawled over the antique dolls in an unladylike, abandoned posture. I realized Missy needed a job that would keep her from accidentally damaging something valuable. As I started to remove the sailor from her arms, she let out a wail and clutched at him. "I want him."

"Honey, you can't have everything you want." I took the sailor doll from her. "Come on, be a good girl. Let's find a job for you." I looked around, but couldn't come up with anything. Finally, I started digging in boxes and found a set of flowered Melmac dishes. That plastic wouldn't break if she dropped them on a stone floor.

"Here, you unpack these," I said. She calmed down, serious as she started taking them out of the box, and in order to occupy her further, I gave her a clean rag with which to clean them.

"We'll have a party at Christmas," I said, thinking out loud. "We'll invite Elaine, Hank, Mary, Annie, and Bess can come too. Maybe Scotty will be here. Remember Scotty?"

"I love Scotty. I'm going to marry him," she said calmly.

"He's a fine person, but honey, he's seven years older than you."

Missy turned her head as if she'd heard something. "Listen, somebody is at the door." She tugged on my hand. "Come on!"

$\mathcal{E}$laine's tall figure stood silhouetted against the etched oval glass of the front door. Except for the roundness of advanced pregnancy, she was a naturally slender and graceful sylph.

I embraced her in a hug that also encompassed my unborn niece. Everyone had thrilled at the sonogram that showed Elaine's child was a girl. When we asked my brother, Hank, what he thought, he said he'd be glad to have another one like Missy around. "We'll have enough of both kinds of kids," he'd said. "Boys and girls."

"Am I glad to see you!" I ushered Elaine in and indicated a rather dusty-looking padded glider chair. I sat on a straight back from the dining room. Looking fondly at her, I knew why Hank loved her so much; anybody would.

At first, after they were married, thinking to please Hank, she drove into to town regularly for a full range of salon services, coming back with the sleek look of a Florida panther. Hank, though, weary of business and society women, decided it didn't suit her and asked her to go back to what she was before. She eagerly complied by washing her face clean of makeup and reverting to sun-streaked hair caught up in a Grecian fall.

Now, her tanned skin, sparkling blue eyes, and sheer voile dress enhanced her femininity and made her appear as if she had just stepped from the pages of a romantic twenties magazine. It suited her much better than what my hairdresser, Zarriya, and I tried to do with her.

"You seem to be emanating light," I said with envy. How long until I could wear maternity clothes again and live in anticipation of caring for a new wee one of my own? "Would you like some coffee?" I asked my guest.

"It smells wonderful," Elaine, said, "but my midwife asked me not to drink coffee. She laid her hand over her expectation. "I can't stay long. I'm on my way to pick up the brochures for the children's camp. We've decided to call it 'Creation Camp.'"

"Where's my Uncle Hank?" Missy stood in front of Elaine, laying her small hands over her aunt's.

"He had to stay home, sweetheart." Elaine pulled Missy onto what was left of her lap. "He has lots of work to do." Missy looked perfectly comfortable as she leaned back against the baby-bump. I knelt to pluck the last salad plate from a wooden crate of china and stack it with the rest.

"Oh, that's Grandmother's china," Elaine said. "I forgot how beautiful it was." She held out her hand and I gave her the dish. She examined it as she went on, "Grandmother saved what she could from her housekeeping money for a long time before she could buy this."

Elaine's smile was childlike. "I gave it to Annie to sell when I needed to fix up the campground, and she gave me the money, but obviously, she never sold the set."

"Now you can pay her back and take it home with you," I said with perfect logic.

"I could afford to buy it now, couldn't I?" Elaine's voice held wonder; she hadn't grown used to the idea, after living in poverty for most of her life, that her Cinderella marriage would now afford her anything she fancied.

I wished Hank's and my parents could have known her and that they could meet the new granddaughter when she was born. Yet, they would be happy if Hank and I were to go on from here and raise our families together.

"Have you been feeling okay?" I asked, eager for details of her pregnancy.

"I was a sick at first, and so tired, but now, I feel wonderful!" She patted her protruding abdomen. "We may have half a dozen kids."

"You haven't been up all night with the first one, yet," I teased. "But I know what you mean; I wouldn't mind three or four myself."

I finished taking the china from the box and stacking it on a drum table covered with a spiral patterned, hand-crocheted piece. It fit and suited the table perfectly. I liked simple, handmade pieces like this and knew I would keep this one.

"How are you doing, living out all here by yourself?" Elaine asked.

"I think I'll be okay once I get used to it," I told her. "I'm practicing the names of the plants and animals, as you suggested, and it distracts me from thinking about things I might dwell on. We ran into your cousin, Nick, the other night, and he introduced me to his mom.

"They discovered we'd left Raggedy Ann at the truck stop so he brought her home." I paused; this was home now, and I was beginning to hope it always would be. "He seems like a good man." I took a deep breath. "He's bringing his dog over to protect me at night."

"Good old Zorba." Elaine nodded and started the gliding motion of her chair. A somewhat sly smile curved her lips.

"What?" I asked.

"Nothing. Do you have bread? We could make toast." She steadied Missy as the child pointed her toes and reached for the floor.

"I might give you some bread if you'll tell me what's making you grin like the Cheshire cat." The three of us got up and headed for the kitchen.

"Okay, I always thought you and Nick would get along. He is a good man, but he's so terribly lonely." Elaine said, studying my face.

"I'm sorry, but I have other plans," I said, hoping to fend off her matchmaking impulses. I wasn't ready to tell her about Richard being around. She'd get it out of me that I hoped to marry him and then she'd want to know why I was even thinking about going back to him after what I'd told her.

"You mean Richard," she said. "You thought you could get that past me, didn't you?" She waggled her finger playfully. "You forget what a small community this is."

"You're just too smart," I answered. "But really, sister-in-law, you're a jewel in my life. Few people care and listen as you do, and hardly anyone remembers what I tell them."

"I love you," she said simply. "Now tell me all about Richard."

Missy was playing with the pots and pans from the kitchen cupboard now, so I knew we were safe to talk while I got the tea and toast together. "We ran into him and some other guys at the Crossroads General Store on our way here the other night." I looked down at my feet as I spoke.

"And . . . what's he doing out here?" Elaine asked.

"He got a job on an estate, and I assume he's back to stay. I have to admit I was drawn to him, even though he's not exactly the way I remember him." I got out some bread and put it in the toaster while Elaine looked in the refrigerator for butter and grape jelly.

"In what way is he different?" she asked, setting the two items on the metal counter near the toaster.

"He has been in prison the last couple of years, and it seems to have soured him. But a relationship with him has always had a sort of tangy flavor." I shrugged. "Who can blame him, though; prison must be horrible."

The toast popped up, I reached for a butter knife, and continued. "He didn't pay much attention to Missy, but that shouldn't surprise me after what he said when I told him I was expecting her."

"He said, 'Get rid of it,'" Elaine answered, having heard the story when we first met. "He topped that by asking how you knew it was his. Those were extremely hurtful things to say." Elaine took the lid off the jelly and pushed the jar toward me. "Do you still love him?"

"There's a spark...I don't know." I placed my wrists together with the knife projecting from one hand. "I feel bound to him." I was too ashamed to look at her.

"That's not necessarily love," she challenged.

"Mother believed in total monogamy," I said. "And I do too."

"Bad things happen between men and women," Elaine replied. "And that's why I say we don't have to pay repeatedly for the same mistake. God forgives. Besides, what's to keep Richard from abandoning you again?"

Elaine picked up a piece of buttered, jellied toast and took a bite.

"Hmm, this is good." She gave a little moan of satisfaction. "You make toast like Hank does."

"That's the way Mrs. McGregor taught us," I said. "Cover the bread with butter and jelly--no being skimpy." I thought a minute about her question. "You know, Elaine, you're right. I hadn't thought of that. There's nothing to keep him from leaving us again, but now that I've had counseling and know how to set boundaries, I think I can take care of myself." That was the best answer I could give her.

"I've got to be in town by noon to meet a person whose son is coming to Christmas Camp, and to pick up those brochures I mentioned, but first I'd love to help carry the china in and wash it, so that it will be happy and know I'm coming back for it."

Missy wanted to help too, so when we got back to the parlor, I gave her the melamine dishes to carry. There now; these would be her job for the time being. She could stand on a stool and wash them, put them away, and take them out again and have tea parties with them. She loved to work and I hoped I could make it a lifelong pleasure for her as our parents and Mrs. McGregor did for us.

Once we stood at the sink together, washing and drying the dishes, I mentioned the Christmas party. "I've been thinking it could be a housewarming. "Why don't you bring the Christmas Camp kids over for it? I'm determined to have the house ready by then, and I'll decorate with the old fashioned toy ornaments I found in the attic, plenty of lights and live poinsettias."

"Great! It'll be our Mary's first Christmas," Elaine said. "Won't that be fun? Annie and Mrs. McGregor will want to help. Scotty is coming to spend Christmas vacation with us. We can invite Jim and Monica, too, but they usually go their separate ways with friends during the holidays. Anyway, won't Granddad Ira love playing the patriarch? Did you know that someone once called him a curmudgeon?"

"What did he say about that?" I questioned, not waiting for her answer. "It's his honesty. It can be taken for eccentricity."

I asked how he was doing. He had one stroke and another after Annie had married him so she could take care of him. They were childhood friends and now were spending their second childhood together. When Hank and Elaine married, they built a communal sort of house for themselves on the Sacred Spring property and invited Annie and Ira to live in one of the spacious, modern cabins. Mrs. McGregor stayed on as cook and housekeeper, even though she had been offered a generous retirement. She said she'd go right out of her mind if she didn't have useful work to do.

"The doctor said to let Ira do as much for himself as he could, but we all coddle him, and that's not good. Maybe when Mary is born, we'll have someone else to look after and Granddad can help, too. He'd prefer it that way." Elaine looked stricken. "It can't be easy for Annie, his having another stroke so soon after they married. She loves him with an old-fashioned sacrificial love. I hope I'll be like her."

"You already are, but I wonder about me. It's hard to imagine loving a man that much." I thought about Richard's tall, strong body and couldn't picture him stooped and gray headed.

"I'd better get going." Elaine rose.

The minute she left, Missy and I went upstairs and I opened the laptop in my room. I checked a few financial matters, and then carried it down the hall. What I was after, right now, was my wonderful streaming music to liven up the house. The site allowed me to choose one hundred stations, but I reached that limit long ago, so I regularly gave up the ones that didn't rate with me to try new ones. It was an answer of abundance to a lifetime of yearning for more good music in my life.

Glad I had installed wireless the first thing when I moved in, I selected a Claude Debussy station, and set the laptop on the landing between the second and third floor. With great anticipation, I knelt in front of the camphor-wood trunk with Chinese junks carved into its top and sides. Missy settled on the steps with her electronic learning game and I knew she'd be entertained long enough for me to concentrate on my treasure hunt.

Whenever my daughter became bored or restless at Casa Del Sol, we played, colored, or swam in the pool. I taught her everything I knew about swimming and the life-saving techniques learned on the job at the country club.

To my amazement, one day back at Casa Del Sol, she rescued a young squirrel that missed his footing chasing another young squirrel and fell into the pool. Missy jumped in, swam over, got the squirrel, and treaded water until I could get to them. I was proud of her, but a bit frightened at her sudden move. I was relieved that the squirrel had been too surprised to bite her.

When we set him on cement at the edge of the pool, he zoomed across the yard and up into the tree from whence he had come. We heard the mother-squirrel scolding in a high-pitched patter. It never happened again, so her scolding must have worked. Either that or her squirrel child became more adept at playing tag in the trees; probably the latter.

I drew six quilts from the top layer in the chest and, thinking of the hands that had lovingly created them, took them into a spare room and piled them on the bed. One coverlet was smaller than the rest and I realized it was a crib quilt. It had a geometric design of diamond shapes, circles, and rectangles on one side in pink and circles in circles on the other in pale green.

The hand stitching was so perfect that unless you looked closely and had excellent eyesight, you would think it was sewn on a machine. Thirty-five handmade tassels were so fine and delicate that they danced when I picked up the quilt. The wonder was that after more than half a century of storage, it had only a small amount of damage.

The next layer consisted of boxes made of cloth over heavy cardboard the way hardcover books once were bound. These held dozens of linen handkerchiefs with embroidery and thread-drawn work. The small labels listed color, date, and price per dozen in a tiny Palmer script: Ecru, 1935, $2.95 per dozen; Poppy, 1936, $3.96, and so on.

The cheerful red-orange of the poppy color lifted my spirits and somehow made me feel not so alone. I piled the boxes on the floor, and reached back into the trunk where my fingers touched something cool and supple. I lifted shimmering folds of dove-gray satin and let the fabric slide through my hands.

"Oh, look, Missy, it's a pair of men's pajamas, and they're monogrammed!" She glanced up, but was too absorbed in her game to pay attention. I examined the pajama top from collar to hem, remembering my fabric art class at the private school I attended. Flat-felled seams and bound buttonholes told me it was likely that the same artisan who created the quilts had fashioned the pajamas.

I scooped up a matching sash with removable silver tassels. A dozen pair of pajamas in different shades, for instance: deep purple, antique white with gold trim, and one pair with manly looking hunter green stripes lay beneath them.

I wondered what Richard would think of these garments. He liked the best materials and wore them hand-tailored to his magnificent body, at least while I was paying for them. My hands stilled as, somehow, Nick replaced Richard in my thoughts. What did a wildlife officer like to sleep in? I smiled to myself as I imagined him in ant-print boxers such as the ones I'd seen in Saks' window one day.

The next to the last layer in the trunk surprised me most of all. Carefully folded garments in sizes from newborn to toddler—brand new, handmade, and never worn—told a story of dashed hopes. By this time, curiosity consumed me.

Close to the bottom, I came upon a red leather book that looked like a journal and, as I opened it, I again saw the same genteel Palmer script. It said, *"The private diary of Miss Violet Whitman, 1936."*

I held it against my chest with the same kind of joy I'd felt when, in the summer between fourth and fifth grades, I had discovered Nancy Drew mysteries in the attic. I cleaned dust from the window to let in more light and immediately had begun to read. That place and those books became my secret hideaway.

A journal was even more exciting than Nancy Drew was, of course, but on second thought, I wondered if I might be invading her privacy to read it, even if she had been gone for fifty years or more. I laid it back in the chest. If I were to snoop into her business, she might come back to haunt me. Then, No, I thought, I don't believe in ghosts. When you feel haunted, it's because you have something on your mind that you haven't been able understand or accept.

Maybe she would like someone to care about her and to understand her. I shrugged. Possibly, I could learn something. I'll decide later, I thought, replacing everything except the quilts. I came out of my fog, as out of a deep sleep, and found that Missy had disappeared. I jumped up. "Missy, where are you, honey?"

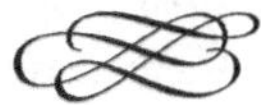

CHAPTER 7

I took the stairs two at a time and ran into the kitchen, heart pounding, and there stood Missy with Bess holding her hand.

"Does anybody belong to this little darlin'?" The older woman wore her pink nylon uniform with the pencil skewered through her graying hair. She must have been coming off the breakfast shift at the truck stop. "You ought to watch her closer," Bess said. "She was on her way outta here."

"Missy, don't run off like that." I took my daughter's hand. "I was just coming to look for her. Thank you."

"Thaddeus said you might need some help," said Bess. "So I came by to see what you need. I make pies like you wouldn't believe. My crusts are brickle as glass."

"I wouldn't want any pies." I sounded as if I'd already hired her. "Well, come in; let's talk about it. Would you like a cup of coffee?"

"Only if you got it made," she said, stepping into the kitchen.

"It's no trouble." How good it would be to have help, so I could get busy renovating the house.

"Those were my mother's dishes. Who washed them?" Bess said, going to the counter where the dishes were stacked. Picking up a plate, she stared at it as if it were a beloved person.

"Dad gave them to Elaine after Mother died. I wonder how they got here." Then, after a pause, she went on, "Oh, I imagine Elaine gave them to Annie to sell when she was trying to save the campground. Annie would do anything for any of us. That lady loved our dad from the time they were in elementary school together, but she never let on because he was married to Mom and she wanted to keep Mother and Father as her closest friends." Bess put the plate down, grabbed a dish-cloth, ran water over it, wrung it, and set to wiping the counter.

"That reminds me; I found Violet's journal in a trunk." I seized the moment. "Do you think it would be all right if I read it?"

"You go right on ahead, honey." Bess puffed air and flapped her hand. "We all read it as soon as Annie found it. Monica and I were just teen-agers. Annie thought it would be a good lesson to us what it would mean to fool around with a married man." When I started to ask another question, she waved me away. "That's all water under the bridge; you read it, you'll see.

"Now remember not to leave dirty dishes out. It'll draw cock-roaches just like that." She snapped her fingers.

What a lot I had to learn and not all of it pleasant. She opened cupboard doors high and low until she found what she was looking for under the sink.

"Here it is; brand new. You just plug it in and it makes the bugs so nervous they can't stay around." It was a new electronic insect repeller in a box. When she unpacked it and plugged it into an outlet, a red light came on and the device began to tick. "I hardly saw any food in the cupboards," Bess said. "Did Nick get that doll over to you last night? We found her in the booth after you left."

"Yes, he brought her over. What a good man he is. I imagine you're proud of him," I said.

"Did my dolly cry?" Missy looked up at Bess.

"No, ma'am, she didn't. She just said, 'Get me back to my little girl.'"

"Thank you." Missy giggled and hugged the doll, which she had brought downstairs.

"Nick's the best man in the whole world as far as I'm concerned," Bess simpered.

"We appreciate him bringing Raggedy Ann home." She liked compliments for him so much it made me feel good to give them. "He was such a comfort—but I thought you called him 'Thaddeus'?" Although I didn't dare use the old-fashioned name myself, I enjoyed hearing the love in her voice when she said it.

"I call him 'Nick' since that's what he'd like me to do around other people." Was it my imagination or did her ample chest sparkle with medals for having reared such a fine man.

"Don't change what you call him for me," I begged.

"You like him, don't you? He likes you. When he came home from the wedding, he said you were the prettiest thing he ever saw and smart as a whip."

"We didn't have much time for conversation at the wedding." I offered a disclaimer, but I was pleased at her kind words.

"He didn't say that all at once, a course." She shrugged. "He don't like to talk about feelings, but he mixed it in with stuff about his dog and his job. A mother learns to understand." She looked me over like a stockwoman evaluating a horse at auction. "He was right, as always. You look just like an orange-juice ad, and I can tell you're smart by them green eyes."

"Not smart enough to look after Missy and get this house finished at the same time, I'm afraid." I smiled at her.

"I wouldn't worry about it, if I was you." She cocked her head to one side thoughtfully. "I can use a microwave if you want, but I don't need one to put some meat on your bones. Nick eats tons and never gains an ounce. He's always been skinny. The boys in school called him 'Bones.'"

"All my life people have been trying to fatten me up," I replied. "I've always had a small appetite, though." We'd have to deal with this fat-thin problem, but that wasn't important right now.

"You got some other pretty dishes, too. See, here's some Depression glass." She opened a cupboard door to reveal shelves full of transparent peach, cobalt, green, and amber dishes etched with patterns, each color on a shelf of its own.

"Aren't they lovely?" I said. "Can you tell me anything about them?"

"They've been here all my life," she said. "Annie used them for special when we came to visit. She collected them from folks she knew and from old houses that were being torn down. She found one set in a cupboard with a pigeon nest that had newly hatched squabs in it."

"Are they from the time of the Great Depression?" I asked, fascinated.

"Yes, the dishes were common enough because the Quaker Oats company put them out. You could get a piece in every box of oats. Movie theaters gave them out, too. Back in those days, businesses had to do whatever they could to get customers." Bess closed the cupboard. "Grandma always said, 'Don't spend all your money in one place.' That meant, share what little money you had to spend among the stores in town."

"These beautiful dishes have probably risen in value," I suggested.

"Oh, yes, you can hardly get it nowadays. If you think you might like to keep it and use it, I could get it cleaned up for you. There are some great dinner cloths and lunch cloths in the linen closet too. We could set a real pretty table if you were a mind to.

"We have silver, crystal, and good linens. Though those don't strictly go with Depression glass, but do you want me to get them out?" She had already removed the vinyl tablecloth and was floating a snowy tablecloth onto the table.

"Yes," I breathed. "I'm trying for Shabby Chic and this is perfect. Do you know what that is?" I asked.

Happiness floated in me like a red balloon. What a miracle that she was as enthusiastic about the house and its contents as I was. She poured coffee into amber cups and set them on matching saucers.

"What do you want to drink, sweetie?" she asked Missy.

"Chocolate milk and cereal." Missy climbed into a chair and knelt so she could reach the table. She had recently decided to reject her booster seat. "And cookies." Her face lit with anticipation.

"Tell me about yourself," I invited as we settled down. "I think that's the proper thing to do in a job interview."

"Mama always made us children work from the time we was the size of this little one here. We loved work, because it made Mama laugh and sing."

"You mean housework, of course," I broke in, impatient to get to the meat of the matter.

"Housework, and..." She took the pencil out of her topknot and scratched her head with it. "I worked in nurseries, too."

"Plant or child?" There were many fern nurseries in the area, so it was a reasonable question.

"I love green things and babies, and I've worked with both. I've been a cook and a waitress; I bake the pies and cakes for the truck stop. I've picked oranges and grapefruit. You know why they call them *grapefruit*?" She didn't notice me shaking my head, but rolled on. "It's because they grow in clusters like grapes. I worked at a fruit-packing house, too.

"I have *born* four children of my own. Thaddeus is my only boy. I was thrilled to have him after three girls, but when they were small, the girls fought over him. I wouldn't say they spoiled him exactly, but he was their doll sweetie until he got big enough to tease them and then all you-know-what broke loose."

"It sounds like you can do about anything." I looked into her earnest blue eyes as I spoke.

"Yep," she said, rising and starting to clear the table. "All the Nicolaides tribe can." She paused mid-stride after she set the dishes on the counter and whirled around, surprisingly light on her feet. "Maybe I better go to the store, and if you want, I'll take the little lady with me."

Missy climbed down from her chair, perfectly willing to follow the stranger.

"Come on, little sweetie." Bess extended her hand and Missy reached for it. "We'll get the stuff to make chocolate-chip cookies. You like nuts?" She was so excited she could hardly contain herself; it wasn't hard to see that she felt working in a home where there was a child was vastly preferable to a smoky, smelly café full of noisy men.

"She doesn't eat nuts," I said. "She thinks they're seeds, and when I start to explain that they're not, I realize they are. It's especially hard to persuade her to eat sunflower seeds."

"Okay if I go out the front? I ain't seen the inside of the house since Annie and Ira moved." She started off and I picked up some of Elaine's china to return to the parlor. When I set the stack of plates on the drum table, they shone as if to say "thank you for the bath."

"Ira is your dad," I said, and she affirmed my statement with a nod. "Is everybody related to everybody else around here?"

"Hmm." She lowered her head and put her finger on her eyebrow. "Elaine's mother, Monica, is my sister. You probably met her at the wedding. Aren't she and I different, though? She has an itch for city lights, but me, I like the home folks, and when I look out my window, I want to see woods, not high-rises."

"It's taking me a while to get used to the woods," I said. Somehow, I could be honest with her and know that she wouldn't judge me.

"Nick can play that upright piano over there in the corner." She flitted from one subject to another like a butterfly sampling flowers, and it was all right with me. I knew she'd leave soon, but wanted to keep her here a bit longer. Missy went over to the cradle and started to look at the dolls, so I knew I'd have to let the two of them go before my daughter decided to pick one up.

"It's probably out of tune," I said, but by the way she cleared her throat and twisted a button on her uniform, I could tell she was slightly offended.

"No, ma'am. In a way of speaking, miss, that piano is already his. He tunes it good and keeps it nice for our Sunday mornings that meet right here…well, we did until Annie moved away." She sighed. "Nick plays it sometimes when he gets lonesome. He's been earning it so one day, if he ever gets a place of his own, he can take it home."

Several antique chairs sat in a semicircle around the piano. How fascinating. I realized I'd known a lot of people, but none as intimately as they all knew each other here. This would be a good place for a home; all I needed was someone to play the daddy.

"How was Nick earning the piano?" I asked, intrigued.

"He's been refinishing the foyer and the staircase, but he's almost done with that. He could get that fireplace out for you if you wanted.

"What fireplace?" I asked.

"He likes a fireplace," Bess went on without answering, "and doesn't mind chopping wood and keeping one going on a cold evening. We had one when we lived in our house with our family. Their daddy was still around then."

She looked at the floor. "He was a railroad man, you know. He was a good man and a good daddy." Missy tugged at her skirt, and Bess picked her up. "We best be going so we can get back."

Now I had a question about the fireplace and another about Sundays. She was on her way, so I quickly chose one and asked it. "How many people do you have in your congregation?" My church in town was so far away … "If you don't have a place to meet, you could come back."

"Let's see." Bess stood, holding Missy. "Nick's friend, Emilio, and his sweet little wife, Serena, and Dan the preacher—he's about my age." Her plump cheeks suddenly infused with roses. "Then that little family that moved in down the road. We get a few migrant workers in the winter and I do a Sunday School outdoors on good days, upstairs on bad ones. I believe that kids need almost as much help knowing how to treat each other as they do getting to know Jesus." She ignored my nod and went on. "All told, we have about twenty people."

"Nick heads up the music?" I didn't want to encourage him as a suitor, but there was nothing wrong with being friendly.

"He made a vow to never play anything except Christian music." She resettled Missy on her hip.

"I like sacred music of all kinds; classical, the old hymns, gospel, and jazz," By now, we had arrived at the door, which I opened so they could pass through.

"That's all right then," she said with satisfaction. "Nick and I do the church music together. I play them bongo drums over there in the corner. We inherited our ears from Mama; in fact, it was Mama's piano." Missy patted her face. "Yes, we're going, little one," she said. "Now, what all do we need from the store?"

"Get whatever you feel like cooking." I handed her a fifty-dollar bill.

"Oh, my goodness," she said. "I won't need that much."

"It's all right; we'll sort it out later." I waved her away.

As soon as they left, I decided to have a break while I could. I ran upstairs to the old trunk and retrieved the journal. Then I went outside and down the soft pine-needle path that wound away from the back door. Large-leaf Pothos, ferns, and long grasses rimmed the mossy steps that went down to a garden of daylilies and a shady arbor with a porch swing in it.

Thrilled with the solitude, I sat and drank in the beauty of the sky framed by the arbor's edge and the abundant plants surrounding me. Sighing, I wiped away flakes of dried leather that stuck to my fingers from the book and opened it. My heart tap-danced as I realized I was about to get a peek into the hidden life of a woman from long ago. Could we possibly have anything in common; a point of empathy, perhaps?

CHAPTER 8

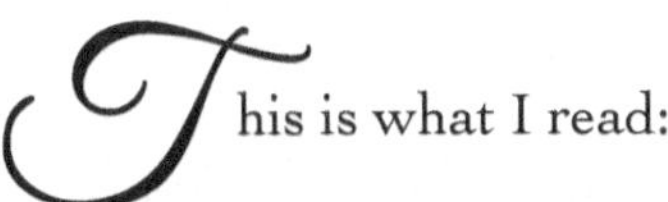

his is what I read:

Texas 1935

My father is a carpenter and my mother a seamstress. They're dear people who love me very much, but they'd be devastated if they knew what I've been doing. It's not that they didn't raise me right. They took me to church every time the doors opened, knelt by the bed and prayed with me every night, read the Bible at breakfast ... But now I am betraying them—and their God.

I'm writing all this down in my diary because I don't have anyone to talk to. My sis, Clara, is no help. When I told her about Paul, she said I'd have to give him up because he's married. You might as well tell Niagara Falls to stop cascading as to tell me to end the sweet agony I experience every time he comes near me. The wonder is that he feels the same.

His wife doesn't understand him. How could she? She's old, at least thirty-five, and wears her hair like a wreath of sausages pinned around her head. She trusses herself in a fitted suit, usually gray. If Paul ever tried to pinch her, the way he does me, his fingers would slide right off her armor.

He's bored with her, says I'm much more exciting...and prettier, even though no one has ever called me pretty before. I have narrow hips, and my bosom is on the flat side. My face isn't bad, but I wish I didn't have a Roman nose. Anyhow, Paul thinks I'm pretty. By the way, he's only a few years younger than his wife, Gladys, is but he says he's young at heart and it is so true. He's always getting himself into mischief.

His father, Mr. Henderson, comes to work every day from eight to six, and it makes him angry that his son would rather be out riding his beautiful stallion or zooming around the countryside in his Auburn Speedster than tending to business.

Just think! If I hadn't gone to business school, I'd be stuck in the sewing room with Mother and Clara. I hate sewing, but love typewriting. Now I'm at hand when Paul comes in. If his dad's not around, he sometimes whisks me away, to "run errands" for the business. We to go a place where...

The next page was ripped out, and from then on entries were erratic. I thought I knew what Violet was going through because it had been the same for me with Richard—the excitement, the obsession, the terrible guilt—though I didn't think Violet had gotten to that part yet. All this happened many years ago, and Violet eventually got old and died.

Nevertheless, her journal made her seem as real to me as anyone currently in my life. I feared for her. I still don't know how God could stop an attraction that strong, even if you wanted him to. Never again would I place myself in a similar trap, no, not even if I had to marry Richard in order to make things right. I read on, anxious to discover more about this mysterious Violet.

Mother and Clara work full time in the sewing room at the factory. It's a waste because they are true artisans who can do anything with a needle and thread. It isn't fair for Mother to have to spend six days a week hemming handkerchiefs and staying up until midnight, making clothes for me.

Clara helps Mother and makes her own clothes, but I'm all

thumbs so I do the household bills and other chores to make up for it. I do love the sprigged voile with the tiny lavender flowers they made. They are such fine seamstresses, they had no trouble with the wide collar that floats over my shoulders like a small cape. Father says the dress isn't decent, but it is. Fetching, too. I saw Paul peeking at me as we walked out of church Sunday. I sit as close behind him as possible in the service, and stare at his broad back. My parents sit with me, however, so I am careful with my glances.

I wore the lovely hat we bought on sale at Finklestein's for twenty-five cents at the end of the season. The smoothly woven straw won't break my fine hair when I wear it. Mother added a small bunch of purple velvet flowers and a grosgrain ribbon around the brim, but in church, the man behind us asked me to remove it because he couldn't see the preacher. When I asked him later, Paul said he loved it.

Father gets quite a bit of business from the country people because he's so good at making coffins and not charging too much. He had a case last week where a girl was charred in a car accident. In order to make her look good for the funeral he spent the night in the basement, peeling off the burnt skin, bit by bit. When they saw what he had done, they were extremely grateful. I shudder to think of it. Thank heavens he never asks me to help him.

Our vocations place us on a lower social level than Mother would like, but that will change when I marry into Paul's family, which is one of the most prominent in town.

I'm saving up to have a dozen pair of silk pajamas made for him, but I won't ask Mother to make them, because she'd want to know whom they were for. Mildred at the factory will run them up for me. She can keep a secret. Clara includes me in her prayers, but I don't want prayers — I want Paul.

I looked up from the journal and saw that clouds were gathering, but decided there was time to explore my surroundings. As long as Missy was with Bess, I wouldn't have to watch her so closely, but I was anxious to get back to the house. All that furniture crowded into every available space, the dust, and the looming chores that kept me from doing much of anything else were giving me claustrophobia.

That was the direct opposite of the agoraphobia, which had made me afraid to venture out. Maybe I was just contrary by nature, but perhaps after my mood swung one way, it could sing half way back, and I'd be normal. Eventually I would be well.

I wandered down the trail, which meandered beside the roped-off swimming area, which reflected the sun in spots. Through the water that was clear as a windowpane, I could see fish swimming on the bottom of the spring.

Usually, we Floridians can't tell if a November day will be hot or cold, although the worst of the heat has broken by then. Today, shade from trees along the trail did little to diminish the muggy heat, so in a spontaneous burst of enthusiasm, I stepped out of my sandals and jumped into the water. I'd change my wet shorts and top when I got back to the house.

The water, even though it was seventy-two degrees, felt shockingly cold, so I kicked off the bottom and swam fast to get acclimatized. Then, after half an hour of laps, an arched bridge caught my attention and I ascended on a stairway that came out of the water.

As I stared into the glimmering depths, a wave of euphoria swept through me. Life was good! Shame was behind me if I could just focus on forgiveness and finish with my panic attacks.

My precious daughter was healthy, I had a wonderful old house to renovate, and new friends in Bess and Nick. Even better, I might somehow get a chance to make things right with Richard.

Suddenly, I tensed as I heard something crashing through the woods on the other side of the bridge. I leapt to my feet and looked everywhere, and then saw that it was a beast or savage of some sort, coming at me through the woods like a Bigfoot gone berserk.

Just in time, I realized it was a man in a loincloth with no shirt, and a band around his forehead that held back long, shiny hair. Not wanting to draw attention to myself, I stood motionless. Should I scream for help? Who would hear me? By now, I had begun to shake uncontrollably. The man spoke and I finally came to my senses. Richard!

"I like your outfit," he said. I was dismayed when I looked down to see that my *outfit,* as he called it, consisted of a damp shirt that revealed every line and curve of my body. I crossed my arms over my chest. He reached for me, but I stood my ground by giving up my cover to push on his smooth, hairless chest. His lips held a sardonic smile that matched a cocked eyebrow.

"You're dressed funny too," I stammered. When I calmed down, I saw he was wearing not a loincloth, but only a pair of camouflage shorts.

"My place is right down there through the woods," he said. "Would you like to see it? The property backs on yours, and we wouldn't even have to go around by the road." He pointed the way.

"No," I said, but my fear was beginning to turn into something else, something like yearning for other times. I took a steadying breath and wondered what Dr. Louise would advise me to do. Then it came to me. She'd say I needed to stop and think about what I really wanted as an end result.

In my mind, I heard her say, "You don't always have to follow someone else's agenda." I mentally shut out the sight of Richard's questioning look, and I prayed, Dear Lord, I don't want to give in again, not this way. In a sudden epiphany, I recalled my vow never to let him take advantage of me. This time he'd have to marry me first.

He grabbed my shoulder and his lips came down, sudden and rough. It had been a long time since anyone had kissed me, but... He growled deep in his throat, the sound of a starved animal defending its meal.

Suddenly, in the midst of whirling emotions, there came the sweet, pure trill of a forest bird. I searched the trees and found a blood-red cardinal with his head cocked and beady eyes looking straight at me as if inquiring if I knew what I was doing. I pulled away from Richard and gave him my meanest look, the one he had said would make a grown man cry.

"You can't do this to me again," I said.

"But, babe," he said. "I'll take care of everything; no one will ever know what happens between us."

I looked down at my bare feet and shook my head.

"Why not?" He placed his fists on his hips and glared. "Is it more of that stupidity about a man not buying the cow if he gets the milk for free?" He frowned. "Come on, babe, what century do you think this is?" Once again, he tried to envelop me in his muscle-bound arms.

"I hated myself so much after you left!" I said, stepping back. "We'll never be involved again unless…" There! It was out. Now stubbornness would require that he dig in his heels and resist in earnest.

"Okay, I'll buy the cow." He shrugged his shoulders as if it didn't matter one way or the other. "You satisfied now?"

"What?" I gasped, immediately biting down on my lower lip. Something was wrong; he couldn't change that fast without an underlying, underhanded plan. I knew him at least that well. "Why would you want to do that?"

"You've still got what I want, and I want it bad." His capitulation was too sudden, too easy. He smoothed his hair, poking stray locks back under his sweatband.

Questions niggled at the back of my mind like worms burrowing through a tomato. Was it that he couldn't resist me, or that he loved me and wanted to spend the rest of his life with me—or was it something else? A daughter of wealth is brought up to be suspicious of everyone.

"What do you really want?" I affected my most business-like squint, congratulating myself for asking reasonable questions when, increasingly, all I wanted was to be held.

"Come on, Jean, you said you wanted to get married." He lifted my chin to tilt my head back.

"I'd have to think about this," I faltered. "Don't pressure me." I backed down the bridge toward the bank.

"I'll come to your house tomorrow night. Now that we're engaged, things are going to be different." He raised his voice slightly as I moved away from him.

Engaged? I started running as if the devil himself were after me and soon arrived breathless at the arbor again--without my shoes. What now? Wasn't that my dream, a permanent connection with Missy's natural father, more children, a real home?

I shook my head, wondering whether I'd actually ended up promising to marry Richard or not. I walked slowly up to the house where, at the back door, I lingered to watch the dark clouds scudding across the sky in the oppressive afternoon heat. The wind rifled the tops of the trees and a mocking bird flew fast over the house,

screeching as if it were trying to warn about the storm and outrace it at the same time.

I heard a car and rushed around to the front of the house to help Bess and Missy unload groceries. The vehicle, however, was Nick's, and as I watched him get out and let his dog out the other side, I shivered inside from excitement.

"What are you doing here?" At least I had the good sense to play it low-key as I sauntered to the truck and reached out to scratch the dog's silky ears. Zorba's tail beat a happy rhythm

"I'm tracking a poacher." Nick took an aggressive stance, frowning deeply. Goose bumps sprang up on the back of my neck.

"Well, it's not me. Please don't look at me like that." My voice came out sounding shrill and anxious. His glare continued to scorch my soul.

"Let me show you something." I wanted to sympathize, but I shrank from seeing whatever mangled creature he had found and his anger frightened me.

"I don't want to see it," I said.

"Look at this." He lifted a bundle that looked like a feather duster from the back of his vehicle and laid it on the ground. It was a red-tailed hawk, beautiful even in death.

"The poor thing. Who could be so cruel?" I bent to touch the soft feathers, but my hand came away with blood on it. A gush of acid rose in my throat, making me afraid I'd throw up. I swallowed hard and jumped up with my hand outstretched to avoid smearing my clothes.

"I've got to go clean this off," I said, hurrying toward the house with Nick striding behind me. I looked back to see Zorba pick up the bird, because that's what Labrador Retrievers are supposed to do. Nick went back to replace it in the truck bed.

CHAPTER 9

When we were both in the kitchen, Nick slumped into a chair; he was calmer now. I dried my hands, and turned to look into his face. All my concerns about Richard flew in a big *whoosh* as I took a deep breath.

"Would you like coffee?" I asked, trying to get things on a lighter footing.

"Made over the old grounds?" he said, going to the coffee pot while bringing a sense of humor into play. He pulled mugs from the cupboard. "Did Mom suggest, yet, that you do that? She says, 'waste not, want not,' at least three times every day." He poured the coffee and turned the handle of the cup toward me.

"I admire your mother's frugality." I took it back to the counter for sugar and creamer.

"Yeah, me too. We never had an overstock of cash, but the Lord always took care of us one way or another. How about you? Did you ever worry about paying your bills?" He turned his chair with the back toward the table and straddled it. His arms rested along the top of the chair as he held the steaming mug in both hands.

"I can't honestly say I have ever given it a thought." My ankles automatically hooked themselves around the legs of the chair. I'd been taught to sit like a lady, but always found this position more comfortable.

My shirt seemed to have dried enough to make me decent, too. "Dad followed his father into an established contracting business," I continued. "His wise investments did the rest."

I watched Nick's face to gauge how interested he might be in my family history, and was reassured by what I saw there. "My brother and I caught a strong case of workaholism from our parents, just as you did from yours, so we've always worked at something. It's sad that so many have to go without basic needs being met. We can't fix all that; nobody can.

"Jesus said we would always have the poor with us. Nevertheless, we try to help people out with our money. I've heard that it creates character to be poor, but I've never wanted character badly enough to try it. I recently read a quotation that I'm wondering about. 'Limited global wealth is a fallacy. There is more than enough to go around and there are always new ways to create wealth.' I guess you can see my confusion."

"I don't know. I'm not much of a philosophizer, but I know you don't have to be embarrassed about being rich," he said. "God needs people with money." He took a careful sip of the hot beverage.

"Poverty can degrade, too. It depends on the person. I'd want to have just the right amount of money. I don't need much to be comfortable, but if I had a family, I'd want them to have some pleasure in life. I want to help people too." He set the cup down. "If you have enough, many other things can be more important than money, don't you think?"

"Money can't love you back, that's for sure." I said, enjoying his expressed thought. I got up to rummage in the refrigerator with renewed hope that I'd find something for him to eat, but the hot dogs and buns were all gone, and Elaine, Missy, and I had consumed all the toast.

"Love is what matters." Nick's hand crept to his chest and his fingers splayed out over his heart. The sweet and humble gesture made a delicious emotion surge through me.

"Be serious," I said, tapping the back of his hand. "Maybe it's not polite, but I like to talk about money. It's something that interests me, and I'm pretty good with it."

"I keep up with my bills okay." He leaned back and stared at the ceiling, and then looked back at me with a frown. "You've got a stain around that light fixture. It means the roof is leaking. Shall I fix it?"

"That would be great, but don't get distracted." Absorbed in the conversation, I gave the stain a quick glance. "The details of your finances fascinate me. Am I too nosy?"

"No." He shook his head. "We don't spend much money on food because we're Bubba's guinea pigs. He's the owner of the truck stop and fancies himself an experimental chef. He calls me a gourmet, which I'm not, because I appreciate most any kind of food. My sisters call me a garbage disposal." He stopped suddenly and took a deep breath "I don't know why I'm talking so much; you seem to have that effect on me."

"It sounds like your living expenses are minimal." I wanted to encourage him to go on. The storm seemed to have rolled by and having him seated across from me in the bright kitchen in my own home felt companionable and satisfying.

"Well, let me see." He stroked his chin. "The truck belongs to the Fish and Wildlife Service, and I get some mileage for personal use. I keep mom's old clunker running.

"For fun, I carve critters and I play music, but neither of those cost anything. The wood comes from the forest floor, and the piano is here. I didn't even buy my own tools because Granddad gave me his." He examined his hands. "Thank God for good health. Ira can't carve or do much of anything else now. He was good; sold about everything he carved."

"Do you have some goals or dreams?" I wanted to know him well.

"Yep." He nodded. "Most of my paycheck goes into the bank for a place of my own. You have a good idea here. It's fun bringing the work of the old craftsmen back to life."

He got up and went over to refill his cup. If Bess didn't come soon, I'd have to make more coffee, or maybe he'd make it over the grounds left in the pot. I had no idea how it would taste, but for some reason, the idea tickled me.

"What else?" I asked. Being here with him made me feel almost giddy, as if I had inhaled a balloon full of helium and had begun to talk in a squeaky voice.

"I want the same things most people do: love, a home, kids, transportation, music." He got up and started for another room. I followed him, hanging on every word. "Actually, there is something in this house I want--eventually." We were now standing in the parlor and he was looking at the piano.

"But that's already yours, isn't it?" I asked.

"In a way… it is." He caressed the smooth wood of the piano bench and sat down to push the cover back from the keys.

I cringed when he cracked his knuckles, and watched as he began to run his long-fingered hands over the keys in a soft glissando. The rippling music soon became, "What a Friend We Have in Jesus," filling the room with a lovely sound.

I sat down to listen while he segued from one sacred song to another. A joyous peacefulness came over me, leaving me slumped like a soft pillow on the old-fashioned settee. When the last melody faded, I roused myself and went to him.

"Your mother says you tuned it yourself. It sounds wonderful." I laid my finger on one of the keys where his touch had recently warmed.

"Even though it's difficult because of the humidity to keep a piano tuned in Florida, a master-tuner taught me some tricks. Besides that, it has an excellent soundboard, so that helps." Our hands almost touched as he, too, caressed the keys.

An invisible cord seemed to pull us toward each other. "Bess said you once had Sunday meetings here," I said in a low voice. "Would you like to do that again?"

"We need to. The congregation has fallen apart since we stopped meeting regularly. Our preacher is still around, though. He works at the Space Center and drove over to be with us on Sunday mornings."

"I think I would love your services," I said. "Missy could come to your mom's Sunday School with other children. She would enjoy that. She doesn't have anyone to play with right now; really, she never has had. Did Hank and Elaine come to your meetings?"

"We shut down about the time they got married, so no, but they might like to if we get going again. Our preacher is good. He's so positive and uplifting. We find that everybody is smiling as they go out."

"What kind of projects do you have planned for this house?" I stepped back to keep myself from touching his shoulder, as I wanted to.

"For one thing, the banister in the front hall has been thoroughly sanded, but now it needs several layers of varnish."

"Bess mentioned something about a fireplace, too," I said, nodding. Suddenly, we heard a high piping voice and a lower, grandmotherly one. When Bess entered the kitchen and saw Nick, her voice rang with gladness.

"There he is! How's my boy?"

"Hi, Mom." Nick squeezed her, and then Missy said, "Hug me too, Daddy." I blushed as he bent to scoop her up, and hoped he hadn't heard what she called him. In case he had, I said, "She's a bit confused right now."

"We have to tell you about our trip to the store, don't we, little darling?" Bess inquired. "But first, help us bring in the groceries."

When Nick carried Missy out, I sighed with contentment. Maybe I'd have to share my daughter, but I'd gained a dog, a friend, a house-keeper, a grandmother, a carpenter and--a cousin, or something. Warmth and security surrounded me. I was beginning to like this way of life.

"Did you buy animal crackers?" I asked Missy as we all pulled foodstuff from Bess's grocery bags. Missy's head bobbed up and down.

"I knew it." I half turned to grin at Nick as I opened the refriger-ator door to put away a carton of eggs. We now had cheese and lunch meat, too, so Bess and I threw together some sandwiches and opened a bag of potato chips. After the blessing, Bess told us more about her job, Nick's job, and some about the owner of the truck stop. Too soon, Nick had to leave, so Bess and I got back to housework.

Missy and I slept late the next day and when we went down to the kitchen, Bess was just sliding a huge turkey into the oven. "It's one of the cheapest meats you can buy," she said. "I don't know why people only eat it at Thanksgiving and Christmas.

"We can make turkey divan, hot turkey sandwiches, and turkey salad. Then we can make soup with the bones. If we had a freezer, I could really save you some money. However, I can take some of it to the truck stop and store it in the freezer there until we need it.

"I'll bake their pies and cakes here if it's okay, so I can keep an eye on little sweetie." She shut the oven door, checked the heat dial, and was already busy removing her shoes, selecting an old dishrag from the drawer, climbing on a chair to dust the upper cupboards before I could take in the idea of having all that meat to deal with.

In spite of her bulk, she was as agile as the goats Missy and I had seen climbing at the zoo. She stepped onto the countertop and stretched to reach the high shelves that were almost to the ceiling in this antique house.

"Here, take these." She handed down some dishes. "First thing, we deep clean, starting with cupboards."

While we worked, Missy made a clatter by stacking and unstacking pots and pans on the linoleum floor. By the time one side of the kitchen was finished, Missy was pulling on my shirttail, asking for her computer learning game, so I went upstairs and got it for her.

I bounded back down into the succulent aroma of roasting fowl. My appetite had picked up alarmingly in the last couple of days. Maybe Bess would succeed at fattening me up after all.

"What else shall we do?" I asked, figuring the kitchen was the housekeeper's territory and she could be the boss. I enjoyed her delight in cleaning and setting things in order.

"You tell me what to keep and what to throw away." She waved her hand expansively. "Now these here straws can go, and there ain't a question about cobwebs. No use for them at all." She gave me a wry look. "But I don't know about these old dishes."

"As for the straws," I said. "Believe it or not, somebody will probably buy them at the estate auction, because they're in pristine condition and it's hard to get paper straws these days. By all means, search and destroy all webs, no matter what kind of spider made them. I'd be happier if spiders didn't exist."

"I expect the good Lord had a reason for inventing them, though." Bess gave the ceiling a swipe and stepped daintily to the chair like a princess stepping down from her coach.

I rushed to hold her arm, but almost caused her to fall as she resisted my interference. These Nicolaides people are so independent, I thought admiringly.

"We can use some of the dishes for everyday," I said.

"Good idea. I'll wash--you dry." She handed me a smooth cotton tea towel with "Monday" and a duck with a spread of ducklings embroidered on it.

Her hands were everywhere, filling the sink with hot soapy water, setting in the dishes, washing, rinsing, and stacking them on their edges in the drainer. I couldn't keep up. The flowers on the plates were faded and had fine crackle lines under the glaze.

They'd been used hundreds of times over the years. Wouldn't it be fun if they could tell stories of family gatherings and of women in the kitchen cleaning up together, keeping track of everyone in the family, and caring — oh, so very much for one another?

"I remember a dish like this from family dinners when I was a little girl," I told Bess, picking up a plate with full-blown roses in the center, rimmed by a dozen shallow cups. "This one is for deviled eggs. I wonder whatever happened to it."

Missy lay down on the kitchen floor and went to sleep, so I carried her upstairs to her bed.

CHAPTER 10

When I returned, Bess had found a set of four tumblers with bubbles trapped in their wavy glass. "You'd only want to keep those if you are sentimental about that kind of thing," she said. "They ain't even made right." Hand-painted girls in blue dresses pranced around the sides of the drinking vessels.

"We'll set those in the parlor for the appraiser," I said. They were so primitive that my antiquarian's instincts began to vibrate. "They were probably made a long time ago before the artisans discovered a way to keep the molten glass from sagging as it cooled. You can still see windows in Europe that are wavy on the bottom like that."

"Okay, I'm stopping right after this," she said, dipping them in sudsy water. "So you go on now, shoo!" My presence seemed superfluous, and I was unexpectedly hurt.

"I appreciate your help," she said, as if sensing that I felt rejected. "I'll make you some biscuits before I leave."

"I'll go, but please—there's plenty of food, and I can toss a salad. Won't you stay and eat with us?" I wanted her to stay because I knew the house would be lonely once she left.

"Sounds good, but I have to work the supper crowd for a few more days till Bubba finds somebody to replace me." She set the glasses in the now-empty drainer.

"Oh, no! Then you shouldn't have come today. You need your rest, and you've done so much in such a short time."

"Nothing restores a body's faith in herself like cleaning." She wiped down the counter. "Besides, I enjoy being with you and your little sweetie. I'm the one privileged to work for you, and don't you forget it." She let the water out of the sink.

"Yes, ma'am," I answered, wishing I'd been able to express how much I'd come to treasure her already. One thing I could do was to see that my gratitude showed up in her paycheck, and maybe buy a freezer and a dishwasher. I already knew she wanted a freezer, but I would sound her out about the dishwasher. The work together gave us time to talk, so I guessed I didn't mind doing dishes all that much.

Missy slept through the rest of the morning and I knew an afternoon nap was out. The bookcase looked inviting so I decided to give it a preliminary examination.

The piece was Heppelwhite, or at least a good imitation of it. Several of the books were first editions, in their original, pristine dust covers by classic authors Marjorie Kinnan Rawlings, Pearl S. Buck, and John Steinbeck--books I'd heard about, but had never read.

From their appearance, no one had touched them since they were purchased back when they cost a dollar or two each. No telling what they'd be worth today, but before I decided to put them in the auction, I'd treat myself to reading them. That would be next, after I finished Violet's journals. However, if I liked them, I realized, I could keep them. They would only grow in value.

As I passed the foot of the stairs, I finally heard Missy talking and went up to get her. "We're going to get a daddy," she was confiding in her doll, "but I don't want that mean daddy. I want the nice one—Zorba's daddy." Worry tightened my scalp. She wasn't as confused as I was; she knew who she liked and who she didn't.

Please take away the obsessive part of Richard's nature and make our relationship what you want it to be, I begged my heavenly father. Make us a real family. I sensed the plea winging its way to him and thanked him in advance for his answer, whatever it might to be.

Missy needed consoling when she found Bess gone. In one day, those Nicolaides people had poured out unconditional love and woven a soft blanket of security around us. I was deeply grateful.

Until suppertime, I pulled tablecloths and doilies from a linen drawer in the dining room and examined them for pinholes, stains, and rust spots. I set aside the ones I wanted to have repaired. Doilies were also called antimacassars; now *there* was a word. Victorian housewives crocheted them for headrests to absorb the men's hair oil that had originated in Madagascar.

While I worked, Missy played an imaginary game of hide-and-seek in empty boxes and behind furniture. Fresh, clean air and shafts of late afternoon sunlight danced through the open window and played over the sparkling kitchen. I would enjoy having guests when I got rid of the clutter and the house had the needed space and light.

A mockingbird trilled, and through the window I watched him leap from the very point at the top of a pine tree and come to rest again in the same spot, as if he were unable to contain his joy. He reminded me of an old saying, "Birds don't sing because they have an answer; they sing because they have a song." I wish I could be like the birds, I thought.

The turkey tasted delicious, but the more we ate of it the more it seemed to grow. By the time our stomachs rounded out like overstuffed pillows, I knew the bird would be part of our lives for a long time to come. Bess would have to deal with it. I couldn't.

"Bess has lots of recipes for turkey," I told Missy, who was busy crawling under the table, playing house, and not interested in my culinary difficulties.

As I placed the dishes in the sink, I decided to order a dishwasher right away. It was one thing to enjoy a chat with Bess, another to be stuck with the chore by myself. After I finished washing and putting them away, Missy and I went out on the porch to enjoy the sunset.

"Read to me," Missy requested, snuggling against me on the swing. After five repetitions of *The Poky Little Puppy*, I was ready for her to go to bed. We went upstairs for alternated drinks of water and trips to the bathroom session until she finally settled down, looking at the stars on her ceiling projected by the night light I'd brought from home.

As soon as I got her to sleep, I wandered outside again, sat down on the swing for a while, got up, and walked around the house, and finally, came back to sit on the top stair and gaze out at where the sand road dipped and rose, and dipped again coming toward the house.

It would be wonderful, I mused, if someone big and strong and smelling of after-shave was here to hold me in his arms. It would also be grand if he had an outdoorsy, woodsy fragrance, as Nick did, an inner voice said. The frog chorus clamored as background to my thoughts.

I ached to be loved, and yet, I was so afraid to let go of my hard won and shaky emotional independence and let it happen. Richard's appeal seemed strangely diminished as I recalled sweet, intimate conversations with Nick that filled needs physical encounters with Richard had never quite met.

I slapped at a mosquito that whined in my ear, but only succeeded in hitting myself in the ear. It hurt. Clouds trailing silver tendrils of mist swirled across the moon. I snapped the porch light on and as I sat in its glow with my arms around my knees, a flight of small moths began tossing themselves against the porch light

Two yellow orbs swam into view through the fog--some kind of mirage or perhaps a southern version of northern lights. I heard booming hard rock music. So no, it was just a car, but not Richard's or Nick's.

I ran my hands through my hair and smoothed my shorts as a rusty old Nova pulled into the yard and continued chugging for several seconds after the ignition went off. One of the men from the general store stepped out on the driver's side. He looked like a weasel in a cowboy hat. He waited until another man, who turned out to be Richard, emerged, then threw an arm around his shoulder and the two of them staggered to the porch.

"Say 'hello' to my buddy, Raker," said Richard. Close up, they smelled of alcohol and something else, but it was certainly not after-shave. "Aren't you going to ask us in?" Richard leaned on the other man and steered him toward the front door.

"Let's stay out here," I answered, having learned a few subtle self-defense tricks from my therapist. "It's cooler."

"Got any beer, for me, babe?" Richard said, too loudly. "Raker's driving."

"No beer. Go ahead and sit down." I hoped they would follow my example and get no closer to the front door than the steps. "Are you from around here, Mr. Raker?" My heart was thudding, but I spoke to him as a good hostess should.

"Yes'm, me and my daddy live back there." He thumbed at the woods. "That's how I met up with this here dude. I was out rabbit hunting and near about shot him. Didn't I, man?" He sank onto the step below mine, looking at Richard for approval.

"You sure did, old buddy." Collapsing into the space on my other side, Richard laid his hand on my knee in a familiar manner that infuriated me. I was trapped between the two of them and my mind searched frantically for an escape, while outwardly I remained calm.

"Now here's what we want to talk 'bout." Richard slurred his words. "We want you to go into business with us."

"Business? What kind of business?" I asked, lifting his hand away and dropping it on his own knee.

"Import-export." Richard's head bobbed with tipsy sagacity like a doll with a spring in its neck.

Raker started to laugh, but Richard leaned across me and shoved him with the heel of his hand. "Shut up!" he yelled into the same ear I'd hit going after the mosquito.

"Importing and exporting what? I'd have to know a lot more about it than that," I said. Outside the circle cast by the porch light, the shadowy trees loomed like a platoon of hooded executioners.

My foot jiggled with impatience. Should I make my excuses and go? No, better not. I didn't want to risk drawing them into the house where Missy slept, and where I hoped to rest unmolested later on. Both of them exuded the nervous energy of caged panthers. A wrong word or move and I'd no longer be in control--if indeed I were now. Too bad Nick had Zorba-duty tonight. I'd bet a tooth-bared growl would scare my unwelcome guests away.

"What if we asked you to go to the bank and get a loan for our project?" Richard asked. "You get the money and we'll take care of everything else; no need for you to worry your pretty little head about a thing." They looked at each other and snickered.

"You want me to draw money out of the bank and hand it over to you, no questions asked?" I shook my head. "That's not going to happen!"

The sound of another car muttered against my eardrums. It had to be Nick this time.

"Maybe we can discuss this tomorrow?" I wasn't looking forward to Nick and Richard being in the same place together. "I do business better in the daytime."

"You're uptight, babe; let me massage your neck." With one hand, Richard started rubbing while Raker watched with a hungry look. "Relax, babe," Richard whispered. "Let yourself go."

"Stop!" Here were the strong male arms I longed for, but they no longer seemed remotely appealing. In a moment of dead, cold stillness, I heard the car again.

"Please go." If I could just get them out of there.

"Why? Is that tree hugger on his way?" Richard lifted his head to listen and I recalled that he was a bit deaf in one ear.

He grabbed my arm and squeezed hard and I felt hot anger pour from his body in waves. Too late, I knew that asking him to leave had only made him more determined to stay.

I pulled my arm away and went to greet Nick as his truck rolled into the yard. I watched as he went around to the passenger side to release his dog. Zorba bounded toward us, but stopped short with raised hackles to bare his teeth and snarl, just what I had always wanted, I thought wryly, but was it really going to do any good?

"I see you've got company." Nick signaled Zorba to sit and the dog grew still, but remained tense and on watch. "Richard and Raker, what are you up to?" Nick sounded polite, but I knew he was watching every nuance of movement.

"Are you off duty?" I asked. It was an inane conversation opener, but I was too busy fending off Richard's hostility to be clever. After all, Nick belonged to that dreaded fraternity called *law-enforcement*.

"I kept hearing screaming from the woods," I told Nick. "as if someone was being murdered. Your office said you'd be right out, but you didn't come.

"I checked," he said, his voice laced with amusement. The other two men were laughing outright. Obviously, for once, they agreed on something, probably my ignorance.

"You have some screech owls out here," Nick explained. "I knew what it was when I heard them. If you're not used to them, they can sound like bloody murder." I nodded as he continued. "But it's a beautiful little bird with rust-and-cream colored feathers. That big."

Long graceful fingers indicated about four inches. "We'd better hope he keeps right on screeching. We're losing too many of our raptors. I found one buried this morning. Zorba nosed it out."

"When I was a kid," said Raker, "my daddy shot hawks all the time, but he was wouldn't shoot an owl; said it would bring bad luck. Daddy says, hawks are a nuisance, though." He leaned sideways against the stair rail.

"It was a hawk," Nick said. "Maybe your dad shot it? It's illegal now, you know." Nick's fists clenched and unclenched at his sides.

"Nah, my old man don't roll off the couch anymore, except to get a beer." Raker glanced at Richard and in that moment, I knew without a doubt that they were the ones killing the raptors and doing it without any trace of conscience.

"Those wildlife people don't pay you much, do they?" Richard asked Nick. I glared, willing him to be polite.

"Mind your own business, Luskin." Nick scowled. "I wouldn't trade my job for all the money in the world. And, by the way, what kind of work do you do?"

"Right now I'm with Stephanopoulos over at the old home place." Richard tried to take my hand, but I moved it away.

"I don't remember your being from around here." Nick stood with his field boot propped on the bottom step.

"That was my folks' estate, but we weren't there much. I went to boarding school and spent most of my summers in Europe." Richard's teeth gleamed in the dull light. I knew he was lying. His father had been a chauffeur and general handyman, just as Richard was now.

"You're Hank's sister, ain't you?" Raker interrupted, looking at me. I nodded wondering how he knew Hank. "He's a friend of mine," Raker said as if he understood my question without my voicing it. "He stops whatever he's doing to talk to me. Real fine gent, your brother."

"How did you meet him?" I asked.

"We had a misunderstanding about a little old gal one time. Later, when I got in trouble for something else, he came to see me in jail. I thought that was right nice of him. He didn't have to do that." Raker nodded with approval.

I understood. Hank was up to his old ways of making friends out of enemies, for which I usually admired him. I had told him about Richard coming back, but he wasn't so free with his friendship there because he knew how badly the man had treated me, his little sister.

CHAPTER 11

*H*ostility crackled between Richard and Nick as they glared at each other in the porch light; Richard still sitting, Nick still standing with one hip sticking out as if he were getting ready to draw down.

I was fed up. Why couldn't they at least try to make conversation like gentlemen? Disinterested in the conflict between the others, Raker concentrated on me. He winked and made faces to show his opinion of the opinions of the others. Any moment, he would stand up on his hind legs and beg for a treat like a trained circus dog.

"Missy was grateful to get her doll back," I said, trying to set a new and friendlier tone. Neither the black knight nor the white one spared me a glance.

"I've been looking for a fireplace since your mom mentioned one." I tried to catch Nick's eye. "Is it behind the south parlor wall?" His only reply was a grunt. Apparently, he felt that if he lost his focus on Richard, he'd lose some kind of competition.

"Did you hear how much the stock market went up yesterday?" That got Richard's attention, but only for a moment. He soon returned to staring at Nick.

Their adolescent behavior made me so angry that I decided to leave them to it. "You can sit here all night, but I don't want any part of it."

The screen door gave a satisfactory bang as I flounced into the house. I checked on Missy then, brushed my teeth, and scrubbed my face. I marched into my room to lay out clothes for the next day. For all my raging, no sounds of departure drifted up from below.

Arranging pillows and a light so I could read, I threw myself onto the bed, but my mind whirled with thoughts that made it impossible to focus on a book. What could I do now? I didn't know whether could get involved with Richard again. Might I prefer a new friendship with Nick? It was plain I couldn't have both.

I didn't want to ignore the fact that Richard was Missy's biological dad, and that she needed a father, but perhaps we needed Nick and Bess more. As for Raker, he was just plain creepy. I wondered if he was the man Elaine told me about who, as a kid, gave her such a bad time on the school bus that she punched him out. If he was, I might try it myself, one of these days.

Maybe I should go back down and sock him right now, and give them all something to think about. The thought brought a sense of satisfaction. Yes, I'd love to try it, but the more I thought about it, the more I realized I didn't want anything to do with any of them.

I lay fuming for another fifteen minutes before I heard a car start, immediately followed by another one. I scrambled to the window in time to see both vehicles pull away, Richard in the lead. Nick had out-waited him, no question how I felt about that.

In the night during my tossing and turning, I heard someone return. When I got up to see who it was Nick's truck was backed in with Zorba's nose projecting from the passenger's side window and Nick, silhouetted by the moonlight, standing guard next to it. I fell back on the bed and into what finally came as safe, peaceful sleep.

In the next few days, Missy suffered from a mild cold. Though it wasn't severe enough for a visit to the doctor, she got me up several nights in a row because she couldn't breathe through her nose. I'd never been good at going without sleep, so the nighttime vigils made me weary.

Why not take some extra time when I went to the bank directors' meeting I had to attend in Orlando? I could stay at the Collier, where Mom and I always went for girls' weekends, and I could sleep, shop, and read. I loved the park, though, now, Living Spring was catching up with it in my affections.

The next morning, Bess and Missy walked me to the shed where I'd parked Mother's old Caddy. I threw my suitcase in the trunk atop a jumble of wallpaper and tile samples. The house would be such a spacious, light-filled home when it was finished that I might want to spend the rest of my days there.

"I'll be back in two days, sweetheart." I lifted Missy, feeling the warmth of her small arms around my neck and the vibrant life in her beloved body.

"Bring me a new book." She seemed unconcerned about my absence. I squashed a pang of jealousy, knowing Bess was only the first of many loves who would claim my daughter's heart. Someday she would meet a man who'd crowd me into the back room of her life. What she needed most, right now, though, was kind people to give her an abiding sense of security.

"You've got my cell phone number," I told Bess. "It's a comfort to know she's with someone she loves--someone I can trust."

"Just get going." She bloomed with a beatific smile. "You already told me a dozen times where you'll be. I have a list of foods she likes and clothes she'll wear. You'll only be an hour away; for Pete's sake, and you can call us anytime or even come home if you want to."

Missy leaned toward Bess, and I handed her over. As I pulled away, the two of them, happily entwined, waved me off. Gaining the highway, I pressed the window button so the cool wind could come in and ruffle my hair. I pressed my foot on the accelerator, turned on the CD player, and started singing along with *La Traviata*, hitting the high notes I could, and letting the official soprano take the rest.

A rush of well-being coursed through me as I remembered the words of my therapist, Dr. Louise, at our last session. "Remember, you will be the main source for your daughter's love needs, so the first thing is to stop beating yourself up and learn to give yourself credit for the good job you're doing now. You made a good choice in going ahead to full term."

"Miss Schaefer, you have the Lily Suite," the desk manager announced when I entered the hotel. The bellhop put my luggage on a cart and took it and me up to the penthouse in an elevator. He opened the door and handed me the card, waiting while I fished in my purse for a tip.

I loved the old hotel's air of gentility and the attention to the smallest detail. Here you were a person, not a number. In the living room, a vase of pink calla lilies complemented the art-nouveau theme for which the hotel was famous, and in the bedroom, a gold-wrapped chocolate lay on my pillow. I opened it and took a bite. Delicious. Eating chocolate in the morning was as much fun as ever.

When Mother brought me here as a small child, I believed the gold-wrapped treats were magic because every time I ate one, another appeared on my pillow. Mother let me have as many as I wanted. I'm probably too strict with Missy, I thought. Someday, I'll bring her here and dazzle her with high living. I had to admit I had never appreciated order and cleanliness as much as I did this day. I had never lived without it before.

Lake Eola Park below was the equivalent of Central Park in New York City, only much smaller, of course, because Orlando was so much smaller. In a final check, the mirror showed a healthy young person in an emerald silk dress and a soft natural straw hat probably much like the one Violet mentioned in her journal, only unlike hers, my hair was strong and coarse.

As I strolled, flags fluttered banner-like all around the lake. What a gorgeous day! Out on the water, giant swan-shaped paddleboats dwarfed the real swans swimming nearby. Adding to the serenity of the scene, a gray heron stood on one leg under a weeping willow that trailed into the rippling water.

I entered the open area of one of the tents and examined a collection of watercolors from which I selected three pictures of children at the beach. The same red-haired girl in each of them reminded me of Missy. As the artist wrapped them in brown paper, she told me the children in the pictures were her daughters. She promised to send the packages to the hotel so I wouldn't have to carry them with me.

Next, a long table displaying wooden carvings that reminded me of Nick's caught my eye. I'd sent the manatee mom and calf to a friend who owned a nature-themed art gallery on Sanibel Island, but I hadn't heard back from her, yet. The work on the table was as good as his, maybe better, if that were possible.

Thinking about Nick made me happy. We laughed together, we understood each other in some indefinable way without having to explain things, and we found plenty of things to talk about. He was a great listener, asking questions and encouraging me. He helped solve problems with my renovation schemes and gave excellent advice on rearing Missy.

Now what could this artist possibly have that he didn't? I quit daydreaming and became engrossed in the carvings. None of them was any bigger than a teacup, some much smaller.

Tiny gray-blue feathers decorated the head of a heron that stood on one leg near a lily pad. It looked so real I could imagine the beak plunging and coming up with a minuscule fish. Another carving depicted the snout of a half-submerged alligator that cut a V in the water as an exquisitely detailed hawk watched from a limb overhead.

I stopped cold when I came to a manatee similar to the one Nick had pared at my kitchen table. How could two carvers have come up with the same work? Had someone copied Nick's creation?

The truth made itself known when I saw the missing artist return. He set a cup of coffee on the end of the table. I wanted to shout, to sing, and to dance, but he didn't look up. Instead, he slipped onto a high stool, picked up an unfinished piece, and started to carve.

The tip of his tongue helped him focus, just as it would any great craftsman. I edged toward him and when I got close enough to see his eyelashes, I quietly said, "You're really good," But my words had an unexpected result.

He jumped and knocked over his mug and coffee flew everywhere. Fortunately, I stood just out of range, so my silk dress missed becoming a disaster. His hand was trembling as he picked up the mug.

"Jean! Where did you come from?" His open and honest face held a passionate beauty I had never before seen in a man. With effort, I stepped back, snapping the unexpected tension that gripped us.

"I'm glad you've decided to share your work. It's the best I've ever seen of its kind." Even though we had just seen each other a few nights before when he dropped off the dog, the joy of meeting unexpectedly widened our smiles. "Where's Zorba?" I asked, looking around.

"To answer your first question, I have an old friend who lives here in Orlando. He was roped into serving on the art show committee and thought he'd shake them up by hobnobbing with some country folks. You'll have to brace yourself for the answer to the next question. Zorba's at the vet."

"What's wrong?" I said, alarmed.

"He got shot." Nick put his hand on my arm to help me stay calm.

"What? How?" I was the one shaking now. It was unthinkable that someone would shoot that sweet big dog. However, Nick had said, "At the vet." That meant Zorba was still alive.

"It's probably those guys that are messing around with the raptors," Nick said. "But they won't get away with it. I don't think killing endangered species is their only crime."

"But how is Zorba doing?" I asked.

"It slowed him down, but it didn't kill him, thank the Lord. He was almost out of range, but they did get him in the shoulder, so the vet wanted to keep him an eye on him for a few days. He tells me Zorba is his favorite patient, so who knows; he might have been craving his company. Don't worry," He stroked the anxiety lines away from my forehead, his touch as light as a bird's wing. "The old boy will be all right." He waved his hand at the table. "See anything you like?"

"I like them all," I answered. I wanted to look at them forever, but I sensed he'd be embarrassed if I offered to buy them.

"You're going to have to make up your mind unless you actually want them all. If you do, they're yours. Anything I have is yours." He threw back his shoulders, proud to be able to offer a part of himself.

"Oh, now, you can't do that," I said. "I didn't mean ..."

"Maybe you'll pick one for now and we'll talk about the rest later."

"All right. I love the heron. Thank you so much. Do you have any idea how good you are?" I asked.

"What are you doing here, anyway?" His tawny gaze and the sound of his voice affected me like deep, healing music and I could tell he wanted to touch me. I just knew it, but instead, he picked up the heron, wrapped it in bubble wrap, and put it into a box the right size for it.

"Your mom is watching Missy, so I decided to indulge in a free weekend." Then I wondered aloud, "Why didn't your mom tell me about Zorba?"

"She probably didn't want to bother you with it when you were setting out for some time off."

"You're right. My idea of time off is reading and room service."

"You have nothing else to do?" He reared back in surprise. "I'd go crazy if I didn't have anything to do." I understood that he wasn't criticizing, but remarking on the differences between us. I deeply valued the uniqueness each of us brought to the friendship.

"Well, I don't have anything to do when I'm staying at a hotel and everything is being done for me." My spirits were rising by the minute as I became high on fresh air, sunshine, and something else I couldn't define. "Would you like to join me for lunch?"

"Sounds great." He gave a nod at the other booth. "Karen will look after the booth. She's gone now, but it's my turn when she gets back."

"I'll stroll in this direction in a while, then." I felt like giving him a good-bye embrace, but that would probably embarrass him and besides, I'd see him in an hour, or so.

CHAPTER 12

My family had celebrated so many important occasions at Chez Louis that when we entered the restaurant, nostalgia threatened to overwhelm me.

"Wow!" Nick said, stepping closer to the antique breakfront in the foyer and smoothing it with his hand. As he moved past me, I caught the clean outdoor scent of wind.

"You smell nice," I said, wondering what it would be like to slip my arms around him and lean against that broad, muscular back. Unlike my country club friends whose muscles were developed by resistance training, his strength came from wrestling alligators and dredging weeds from swamps. I'd never met a man who moved with more grace and economy of motion.

"What you smell is the wild thyme growing behind your house," he said, turning with a smile. "I checked things out this morning before I came to town."

"Ah, Mademoiselle Schaefer, how lovely to see you." Henri, a cliché of a Frenchman with a thin mustache, kissed my hand, then shook Nick's, sizing him up as if he were my dad. "So our beautiful mademoiselle has found a friend of the heart." I felt myself embarrassed, yet wanting his approval all at the same time.

"This way, *s'il vous plait*." He led us into one of many dining rooms and seated us next to a window, which overlooked the lake and its swan boats. Nick swallowed hard when he saw the prices on his menu. Mine had none.

"May I recommend the bouillabaisse; it is the masterpiece du jour." Henri hovered over our table, and I knew we were getting special attention because of his admiration for my family.

"Boo...what?" A drop of sweat glistened at Nick's temple. He could cope with snakes and snapping turtles, but perhaps this plush restaurant was a bit too much for him. I suddenly knew I'd been insensitive to choose it.

"It is a delicious seafood dish from the villages of France where everyone makes their living fishing. Our chef uses the freshest of lobster, clam, and red snapper. But to be honest," Henri hung his head and mumbled, "it is said to have come originally from Greece, sir."

"If it's Greek, it's got to be good!" Nick exclaimed. "Please bring me some of that."

"Would you like the mixed green salad with champignons?" Henri offered.

"Which is...?" Nick looked up from trying to find these things on his menu.

"Mushrooms," Henri said.

"Well, fine, and I guess greens are lettuce, right?"

"Yes, sir." Henri chuckled, warming to Nick's unpretentious manner. "However, we do have arugula in our salad," Henri continued.

"Okay, bring it on," Nick answered.

"Your waiter will arrive *tout de suite*," Henri said, and left.

"Do you eat here a lot?" Nick picked up his water glass and drained it in four gulps.

"We used to come four or five times a year. Dad brought his business contacts, Mother entertained her shopping friends, and of course, our family had parties here." Remembering what it had been like to have a family made me sad.

"What is it?" Nick asked, sensitive to my every expression.

"I'm missing them, that's all." I touched the stiff white napkin to my cheeks, glad I wasn't wearing mascara.

"Yes." He turned his head away to look out at the lake. "Family's best, next to having one special person to love." He touched my fingers in a brief contact as delicate as the landing and takeoff of a butterfly. "Do you have any idea how beautiful you are?" he said quietly.

"What do you do for fun, Nick?" I looked out the window again, wanting to get the conversation back onto lighter footing.

"I catch poachers and put them away long enough so that they forget what a tree looks like." He caught the eye of a busboy and indicated his water glass.

"We found another cache of hawks somebody shot." He paused while the waiter set down large bowls almost overflowing and studded with clamshells. If only we could find the right subject, we might have an enjoyable conversation. He sensed what I was feeling and changed the subject.

"The house has been standing for over a hundred years, but it has no termites and no wood rot. Do you know its history?" he asked.

"Some. Annie didn't have time to go over all of it." Now we were talking!

"I'll finish that banister next week," he said. "I've decided it needs wax rather than varnish."

"You're right," I said. "Wax would let the wood grain show."

"You should have seen it when I started." He rubbed his hands together as if he couldn't wait to get his hands on some more wood. "It was charcoal colored. Smoke from kerosene lamps and fireplaces do that to wood. I sanded it and rubbed it down three times until I began to see something like roses carved into the newel post. They turned out to be the grain of the curly pine."

"It's a beautiful staircase and you've done a great job with it." I settled back to hear a story.

"In the early 1800s, Ben Wakefield met Ellie Schultz on the dock in New York," Nick began. "Ben was embarking for Florida, planning to make his fortune; Ellie had run away because she was pregnant and had no husband. Apparently she was afraid of what her parents would do when they found out."

"It happened even back then—to perfectly nice people, though foolish, maybe," I said, comforted.

"Well, anyway, they liked each other immediately." He smiled. "Ben needed a wife; Ellie needed a husband, so they struck a bargain.

Soon after they left the dock, the ship's captain performed the ceremony with members of the crew for witnesses.

"At the mouth of the St. Johns River, they transferred to a smaller boat, steamed upstream, and came ashore at Living Spring. The St. Johns is the only river in America that runs from south to north, you know."

My gaze followed his fingers, which drew a map on the tablecloth.

"They built a cabin and planted orange trees, and after years of painstaking work, they put in a narrow-gauge railroad that ran from the river up to the fruit-processing shed. That way, they could load citrus from the grove and unload supplies from the boats that brought them upstream.

"Living Spring became a mail stop. Ellie ran the post office while looking after the children they continued to have, keeping house, and working in the groves when the smudge pots needed firing in order to keep the oranges from freezing. Maybe she helped at harvest. Maybe some of the hands or their wives helped her too, but the lady had plenty to do, I'll tell you that.

"She raised a fine family even though they lost that first little girl when a rattlesnake crawled into their cabin and bit her. When they could afford to, they built the big house to keep their children safe.

"Did I mention the fainting couch? It's still there." He paused for my response.

"A fainting couch?" I was fascinated.

"It lives in the room off the parlor," he said. "Here's how that worked. Mail boats carried passengers, and you can imagine how hot it was in the summertime for a lady in her long dress and tightly laced corset."

"And petticoats ..." I made a swipe at my forehead to mimic being overheated. "I read that after most women had been here a while, they went to wearing their shifts or men's pants and loose shirts, especially if they had to work in the fields or groves. I can't blame them; they were among family. Why should they suffer the heat any more than they had to?"

"But," he said. "A lady coming from the north was dressed to the hilt, and after landing, she'd get about halfway up the slope and keel over. It was a regular thing for a couple of workers to get the litter and haul the lady up to the house where they would lift her by her hands and swing her onto the couch in Ellie's office. It was one of those French things, you know…"

"Chaise lounge?" I supplied.

"Yeah, one of those. The last time I was in that room, I think I was about ten, it was still there." He drank from the glass that had been refilled three times.

"That little room is so full I can barely get the door open." I sipped my water too.

"I'll help when you're ready to tackle it," he said. "Ellie's second daughter became a naturalist, and their son ran for state senator. Annie is Ben and Ellie's great-granddaughter. No one but their descendents has ever owned the house, up until now."

"I love old stories like that," I told him. "Can you tell me anything about Violet and Clara?"

He rubbed his chin as he thought, then said slowly, "Violet was a cousin." He paused for memory to serve up the next thought. "She came to Florida from Texas." He bent his head and set about consuming his lunch.

"I found Violet's journal," I said. "Do you think anybody cares if I read it? To be honest, I've already started." I didn't like admitting I was nosy, but I didn't want to be pretentious with Nick, either, with anybody, really. I'd seen enough of *putting on airs* at the country club.

"Annie knew it was there. If she hadn't wanted anyone to read it, she would have taken it with her." He shrugged. "It was all a long time ago, before World War Two."

We finished our meal and Nick pulled a thin fold of money from his pocket. He held it under the table and looked down to count it.

"I invited you. I'm paying," I said firmly, berating myself again for the foolish choice of restaurants. At least I could have made an arrangement with Henri.

"No, ma'am," he said firmly. "You did me the honor of spending some of your get-a-way time with me." He signaled the waiter.

"But I …" I placed my hand over his as he laid the bills on the tray.

"Thanks for making this an outstanding day." Nick squeezed my hand gently in return.

"At least let me leave the tip," I said, fearing he was short of cash.

"Okay, thanks, that's fine," he said. So, I was right, he had spent his last dime, probably the last of his paycheck. I wanted to cover my face in shame for being so thoughtless, but I didn't want to embarrass him further, so I let it go. Maybe I could make it up to him.

On our way back to Nick's table, we stopped to listen to the wonderful calliope sound of the carousel. "Look at me!" shouted a child mounted on an ostrich as her parents waved from a bench on the sidelines.

As we watched the ponies undulate in long, slow gallops, I suddenly recalled how disappointed I'd been as a child when someone put me in a stationary carriage, and how my mother had comforted me by promising she'd never let them put me on anything but a *real* horse again. That was something wonderful about my mother; I couldn't recall that she ever broke a promise. I hoped I could do as well by Missy.

"I'm thinking about carving some life-sized carousel horses." Nick spoke into my ear, close but not quite touching. "Do you think Missy would like one?"

"She'd love it. Come on; let's do some hands-on research." I tugged at his arm like an excited child as the merry-go-round slowed.

"What would the guys at work say if they saw me on this thing?" His eyes twinkled.

"Come on, don't be a stick-in-the-mud," I goaded.

He looked the other way when I bought the tickets, but I sensed that he had set aside his pride because he could see how excited I was about riding the carousel. He looked big on the fine white steed he chose, but he beamed like a small boy until he saw the tears that suddenly ran down my face.

"What's wrong?" he asked.

Smiling, I waved away his concern. It was the first time in my life I had cried without having any idea of the reason for it. I've heard people say they cry because they're happy, though, and maybe that was it. It was plain that Nick was good for me, but I didn't know how to process that insight as it went against all I was striving for.

"Is it something I said or did?" he asked at the end of the ride when he helped me off my pony.

I shook my head and we sat down on one of the benches. He

clasped his hands between his knees and looked sideways at me as I settled next to him, my breath catching in hiccups.

"All right, now?" he asked. "Do you want to talk about it?"

"I'm happier than I can ever remember being." My shoulder fit under the arm extended along the back of the seat, and I scooted closer.

"Oh, I see," he said. "This is how you do happy."

It was then that the thunder boomed to the east of us, and the wind came up. I removed a strand of hair blown into my eyes and suggested, "It's going to rain; don't you need to take down your..."

"Richard's no good," Nick said suddenly. He took my hand and I let him hold it. "I'm sorry. I have no right . . . What you do is your own business." He hung his head.

"You're my good friend, and I appreciate your help." I patted his knee to show I wasn't mad at him. "But you're right; it is my business."

A hurt expression crossed his face, and I knew must try to make him understand. "I plan to marry Richard because I need him and Missy needs him, and because years ago I married him before God in my heart." The words sounded hollow even to me. "You know he is Missy's father."

"That doesn't mean you have to throw away the rest of your life. Haven't you heard that two wrongs don't make a right? Sometimes you have to let go of the past." His face was full of empathy.

"I've had so much shame." Confused, I fingered my bracelet. "Shouldn't you close your exhibit?"

"I'm sorry about the other night," he said. I rose, but he caught me by my little finger and gently held me there. "I stayed because he wanted me to leave; it was small of me."

"No, it wasn't small. You thought I needed protection. It's okay. I was glad you were there."

"Oh, yeah?" He beamed. "Okay, then, yes, I'd best get back. I'll see you soon." He jumped up and gave me a peck on the cheek. "Thanks for introducing me to that Greek seafood, and for the merry-go-round ride." Without further ado, he struck out across the sward, leaving a hollow space in my heart.

CHAPTER 13

$\mathcal{I}$ went back to the hotel to rest before doing a bit of shopping and attending the board meeting. First, I decided to take a bath. Fragrant salts glittered as they fell into the stream of hot water from the faucet as the tub filled. I slid into the hot water and leaned against the back of the tub so that my shoulders began to soak in the relaxing heat.

From that position, my gaze went to the ceiling, which was filled with a stained glass skylight backlit by the afternoon sun. Its pink lilies and leaves glowed against a transparent indigo background. What glory it was, God's handiwork, and the giftedness of man combined.

I thought about how good he was to give humans talents and creativity. I recalled that one of the first people described in the Bible as being a praiser of God was an artisan. However, thinking about his goodness, I also could not help but ponder the hard things and the suffering in the world, as well.

Why was I born in this wonderful country, I wondered. Why did I come into such a good family when sometimes people lived in such misery? It never made sense and I couldn't stop searching for an answer. I knew it wasn't in God's plan for anybody to starve or to freeze to death. The only conclusion I could reach was that a lot of bad

things that happen are the result of poor choices or attacks from unre-
generate people.

Anyhow, I wanted to do whatever I could to eradicate the ugliness
in the world, so I prayed that God would give me ways to help. He
grieves over human sorrows more than we do, I thought. And I
couldn't judge anyone. I had to admit that at times, I chose my own
way over his and the poor results were to be expected.

Lord, I thought, I don't want to serve evil or even my own desires.
I've had enough of doing the wrong things for the wrong reasons, and
ending up miserable. Please show me the way to get your best results
into our lives.

I washed my hair and toned my skin with rose water. A soft terry
robe lay draped over a warming rack. Even though the weather
outside was balmy, the air-conditioner chilled the inside environment
and the warm robe felt wonderful.

I dressed in a shimmery green and turquoise crinkle skirt and a silk
blouse that went with it. Medium-heel business pumps and a jacket
completed my office costume. I didn't believe in dressing like a man
because, well, I loved beautiful things.

The board meeting wasn't until four o'clock, so I had more time to
explore. I knew Orlando had grown in the few months I'd been living
in the country, and the downtown had been mostly given over to office
buildings, so I got my car out of the parking garage and drove to
Winter Park where they had wonderful little boutiques and where my
favorite, privately owned bookstore was somehow still in business.

On the way to the bookstore, the window of an antique shop
offered a good chance to compare goods so I stepped inside. To my
delight, the owner was a friend who had been on committees with me
in high school. As it turned out, he was the auctioneer for the sheriff's
department when they confiscated stolen goods as well as for all
kinds of items purchased with drug money. He also managed estate
sales.

For a twenty percent commission, his staff would handle the whole
process: appraisals, clearing out, cleaning the house, advertising online,
and sales. That was too good to pass up, so we signed a contract there
and then. I would finish going through things myself and then his crew
would come out.

Next, I shopped to my heart's content in the bookstore and the clerk helped me carry my purchases to the car.

It was good to see some of Mother and Dad's old friends and partners. They all treated me as a favored child, but took what I had to say seriously, which was gratifying to a young mother.

Afterward, I drove back to the hotel and allowed the parking valet to take the car away. As I walked up the steps, I saw a man standing at the front desk and the sight made me want to seek a back way in.

He wore a purple sports coat and black turtleneck sweater with a large silver cross dangling from a chain around his neck. A raven's wing ponytail gave him the look of a gangster. There was no way to avoid Missy's father, so I lifted my chin and walked confidently in.

"Why didn't you tell me you were coming to town without the kid?" Richard said as he grabbed me and started propelling me toward the elevators.

"Hang on a minute!" I pulled back, looking around for help. The clerk shot a glance at a man in a dark suit standing by the door. He started in our direction, and when Richard saw him, he released me.

"No problem." Richard showed both hands palms outward and the reassured floorwalker returned to his post.

"Behave yourself." It was my turn to take hold and urge him into a windowed alcove. He sat down on a small sofa—such a big man that he took up most of it. He patted the seat beside him, but I didn't want to sit that close, so I perched on the edge of an adjacent wing chair.

"I couldn't believe it when the sitter told me you were here by yourself. Why didn't you tell me we had a chance to be alone?" He leaned over and took both my hands in his big paws. I tried to pull away, but his grip tightened.

"You went to the house?" I exclaimed.

"Sure," he said. "Why?"

"Did you see Missy? How is she?"

"How should I know?" So much for fatherly concern. "Why can't you sit beside me?" He patted the seat again.

He had a two-track mind—sex and money. I wasn't interested in either right now. I was more in the mood to have my dinner alone and get into bed with a good book. I wished I had ordered room service, but as Mother would say, "If wishes were fishes, we'd have a fine fry."

"Why don't you come upstairs with me?" Richard demanded. "You told me when we went away that you married me in your heart. We're somebody's parents, after all. What are you afraid of?"

"You left me, remember?" I felt my temper rising. "You told me to get rid of our baby. You didn't come looking for me when you got out of prison. How can you expect me to trust you now, after all that? It's just too late. What do you want from me anyway?"

"You are so pig-headed, I can't even talk to you. If you did what I said, there wouldn't be any problem."

"Like what?" I asked, afraid to hear the answer.

"Where do you get this stuff about it being wrong to get rid of a bunch of cells you don't even want in your body? It would be against the law if there was anything wrong with it. Besides, I was just a kid, nowhere near ready to have a kid." He sighed. "But hey, forget all that. Prison taught me that I need the love of a good woman." He fingered the cross on his chest.

"I already knew that." I had the power to erase his sullen pout if I twined my arms around him and treated him like a wounded child. But nothing would ever quench the thirst in his soul. Neither could the rules and routines of "religion." Only a genuine encounter with God could do that.

"The old lady said you were going to be back on Sunday," he said.

"Please don't call her that; she's a jewel." I was tired of this discussion, but not ready to give in or give up.

"You don't need her or anybody else, babe. You've got me." He startled me by suddenly dropping to his knees and saying, "Marry me and make a decent man of me."

I cast a sideways glance at the lobby to determine whether anyone was watching. It was empty except for the desk clerk, who focused self-consciously on his computer screen.

"Would you come back to town tomorrow morning and go to church with me?" I asked him. "And would you consider letting me make an appointment for couple's counseling?"

"I want you to come see where I live. Will you do that?" he snapped, ignoring my questions.

"Why? I asked.

"Simple, birdbrain. I came to see your place, and now it's only polite for you to see mine." He stared at a girl in a tight sweater, miniskirt, and ultra high heels who happened to be walking past the plate glass window.

"Get up and let me go." I demanded, eager to escape.

He stood and assumed that hangdog look I once found irresistible. What kind of a bone could I throw him? Ah, yes, he had asked me to see his place. It might be dangerous to pacify him, but I wanted out of this situation!

"Look," I said. "I'll come over one day this week. Right now, I need to talk to the desk clerk about my bill. You want to pay it for me?" I expected him to be incensed, but he surprised me.

"All right, babe, I'll drown my sorrows at the bar. Can I put it on your tab and we'll settle up later?" He stepped back to let me go.

"No," I said as I turned to leave, but I knew he'd do it anyway. Oh well, I'd settle the bill, even though I knew he'd never pay me back. It was worth it to get rid of him. "Go," I said. "Only one, you hear?"

"Yeah, sure, I understand." He made me furious by giving my breast an almost imperceptible flick. I slapped at his hand, but he was gone.

As soon as he was out of sight, I went over to the desk and asked for three things, security to guard my room, the valet to bring my books from the car, and a light supper from room service. After that, I crawled into my elegant cave.

When I took the time to survey the room, I noted a small but exquisite bouquet of flowers on the table in the dining area and smelled their fragrance. The card said, "Thank you for a fine time this afternoon. Nick." I wanted to hug them to me, all the while thinking what a terrible expense I was getting to be.

Soon I heard a knock at the door and padded over to check the peephole. I saw a distorted view of a compact female in a uniform with a walkie-talkie and a gun on her hip.

I opened the door and we chatted for a moment about men, agreeing that you sometimes had to have protection from them. She looked as if she could do the job and most of my fears melted away as I shut the door, leaving her to do her job. Her pay would be on my bill, but it was well worth it for the peace of mind it spread over me. Supper and books soon followed.

When I finished the thick, juicy chicken salad sandwich on whole grain bread and washed it down with the hot tea, the bed with its soft linens and my favorite nightgown beckoned. I piled up the pillows and in my nightgown and robe started looking through the books I'd bought.

I'd always happily indulged in buying brand new, hardcover books, hot off the shelves. To some, I'd learned, such things were luxury beyond reach, but Hank and I never lacked funds for anything we wanted. As our dad always said, "Enjoy life, kids, you can't out give God."

I could already tell that the new Bible would give me many new and wonderful spiritual insights. I had an ebook reader, which was great for travel, but I so dearly loved the heft, look, and smell of what I called "real books" that I hoped they would never go out of production.

I planned to clear a bookcase for these at Living Spring. The ones I bought for Missy, full of joyful pictures, color, and imagination would go on the lowest shelf in her room so she could take them out and look at them any time she wanted to.

The Bible pages felt whisper thin as I looked for a fragment of verse I'd been thinking about: Psalm 68:6 "God places the lonely in families." Immediately, I thought of our new home, of Nick, Bess, Elaine, Hank, and the rest of the family and what they had come to mean to me.

The decorating books drew my eye next, so I thumbed through them looking at the lovely rooms. Then I read the inside covers and backs of the novels by my favorite authors. Beginning to relax, I picked up Violet's journal, which I'd brought along on my mini-sabbatical.

~

I'm sure Paul is going to marry me, but he seems reluctant to ask Gladys for a divorce. Obviously, she doesn't love him, or understand him the way I do, so why won't she let him go? They've never had children. I don't think she can, but I have begun to suspect that is not the case with me. I went to the doctor and he did a test where he injected some of my urine into a rabbit, waited a few days and then checked to see whether the hormones from my body had made the rabbit's ovaries enlarge. They had. The process interests me; maybe I should have become a scientist. I'll tell Paul about the stork's visit soon, but for now, I'll start working on the layette. Even though I don't like to sew, I do enjoy crocheting, and will make sweaters, booties, and a lovely shawl for taking our little one out in the car.

Mildred, in the sewing room, will make a trousseau for me, pajamas for Paul, and a quilt for the cradle. The material was costly, but worth it. Paul gives me a little money now and then, but he's unaware that I'm spending it on him and our family. Mother says he doesn't come into the workroom any more now that I'm not there. I'll have to be careful; my dear mother is probably fishing for information. Unbeknownst to her, however, I bask in Paul's presence daily in the office. We're quite alone there when his father is out of town.

I'm planning to use a couple of hand-carved, camphorwood chests from China. We receive fabric from mills in Ireland, and send it to China for cutting and embroidery. When the Chinese complete their work, they ship the materials back to us in the chests we ask for. There's a stack of them in the warehouse, and I'm sure I can get a couple of them for a good price.

It's Mother and sister's job to put the finishing touches on everything that comes into the factory. Mildred says she will set aside extra linens for Paul and me to use in our home. It will be such a lovely home that people won't be able to stay away.

I don't know how long any of our jobs will last. Paper tissues, which I think are tacky, are taking over the handkerchief industry. I hear some society ladies use them surreptitiously so they can throw them away immediately instead of keeping used handkerchiefs in their purses until they can take them home to wash and iron them. Men will never use tissues, though. Men like plain white handkerchiefs.

Paul tells me his father is thinking of closing our factory and putting the money into something more lucrative. It seems to me that the movies would be a good place to invest. Everyone likes to go to the show, and see stories about rich people. We can find nothing great about the Great Depression. I wonder when it will end. We'll never have another because the "powers that be" will have learned how to handle the country's money better.

If the factory closes, Mother, Dad, and Clara will have to find jobs. They've always wanted to move to Florida near relatives and if it weren't for Paul, I'd go too. They say it's hot there, but it's hot here too. Maybe it's better if they leave without me. I hope to become a scion of society and they would only hamper me in that.

~

Sensing doom for Violet, yet now ready to find sleep, I set the journal aside. As I snuggled into the comfortable bed, my imagination revisited the wonderful day with Nick. Too bad Richard had to show up at the end of it.

The next thing I know, I'm sitting at a dressing table, brushing my hair, and looking at my dark reflection in a mirror. Behind me, curtains move and a man enters the room through French doors.

Somehow, I sense who the man is. As I lean forward, trying to see better in the mirror, he steps behind me, lifts my hair, and kisses the back of my neck. I start to rise, but catch a glimpse of Missy in the open doorway with Raggedy Ann trailing on the floor.

The man turns away from me, grabs the doll, and pulls its head off with his teeth while Missy screeches with terror. She holds her arms out for me to pick her up. The intruder grabs her and throws her over his shoulder like a sailor's duffle bag. He has hold of me with his other hand. I try to wrench away. I try to touch Missy, I scream, I tremble, and I fight to awaken.

~

I sat straight up in bed and looked around. I realized two things: I was in the hotel and I'd had a nightmare. The dream was a distorted rerun of the time when Richard tried to snatch Missy from Casa Del Sol.

We figured he wanted a ransom to return her. Even so, I persuaded Hank not to press charges because kidnappers could be severely punished and I couldn't believe that he'd hurt her. It hadn't taken long however, for him to get into other kinds of trouble.

The dream reminded me that I had to be a hardheaded realist now for Missy's sake. In fact, Dr. Louise would tell me I hadn't caused any of Richard's problems, and that he had made his own choices and reaped his own consequences.

"Are you all right, ma'am?" The security guard's voice came through the door as she knocked gently.

Once again, I opened the door. I explained that I'd had a nightmare and thanked her for guarding my door. Talking with her helped me calm down.

After she left, I turned on the TV, hoping its noise and color would bring me out of my daze, but I soon realized the electronic paralyzer wasn't going to help and turned it off. Sleep had vanished, so I read until dawn.

The next morning, I went to the church my family had attended when I was growing up. I kept hoping Richard would come, but he never did. Why did I continue to give him the benefit of the doubt?

I willed myself to turn my attention to worshipping God. As we sang, I remembered how much God liked us and enjoyed our asking him for things that we knew were part of his plan. He especially liked us to ask for spiritual insight and revelation. I thought lovingly of the family and friends who had continued to support me even though my life was as scandalous as Violet's.

CHAPTER 14

When I got home Sunday afternoon, I had a difficult time getting Missy down for her nap because she was so excited over the beach scenes with small children in them and her time with Bess, but by the time we'd read every new book, her eyelids were drooping. After that, I organized boxes, labeling empty ones for things to keep, things to sell, and things I would, with the permission of the auction team, throw away.

My antique-shop friend had reiterated what I'd already known, which was that people loved surprising kinds of rubbish. Paper straws, old greeting cards, and vintage postcards were sometimes as valued as genuine *objects d' art*. One of the trunks was full of handkerchiefs, table-cloths, and bed linens that didn't seem like rubbish to me.

Nick said the original owners ordered the furniture from Sears and Roebuck and had it delivered by steamboat. The furniture from that period was dark and stiff, so I decided to sell it and see what I could find in wicker, aged rattan, and other lightweight and light-colored materials to give the rooms a lift and make them feel spacious.

I decided to go with a soft eggshell white throughout the house because my favorite interior designer, Alexandra Stoddard, teaches that white walls will reflect the colors present in the rooms. I'm free to make whatever decisions appeal to me, I thought with exhilaration. I have studied, and right or wrong, it's my experiment. If I don't like it, I'll change it.

We'll have six months out of the year when we can use a large screened porch. How lovely to be out of doors every day while winter winds blow up north. I'll have French doors between the house and the porch so I can open the study to the out-of-doors when I'm using the computer. Missy can roam in and out with her toys and still be in sight. I'll have a desk for my own journaling and drawing and an easy chair big enough for Missy and me to sit in together. It will be my favorite room.

After Missy got up from her nap, I took her to the kitchen and asked Bess to look after her while I showered in the metal shower box installed in the fifties. Thinking of a new bathroom, I wondered if Nick was as good at laying tile as he was at everything else he did. If not, I was sure he could find someone for us.

As I came downstairs in clean jeans and a fresh tee shirt, I heard Nick playing the piano. When I reached them, Missy was on the bench beside him, and Zorba, home from the vet, lay on the floor next to his foot. Bess palmed the bongo drums, keeping up a soft rhythm. It was the first time I'd heard that kind of percussion with country gospel, but it sounded right for this time and place.

Nick's friend, Emilio, stroked a guitar, keeping an eye on the piano for direction as Nick conducted with a nod here and a lifted hand there to signal softening the sound to pianoforte.

Missy spotted me and jumped down to run into my arms. It was the kind of greeting I liked best. I scooped her up and squeezed her until she squealed. She was already wiggling, so I kissed her and set her on her feet.

"Bess and I made a pie for you," she chortled, dancing around me. The music ceased and the drum player came to me, smiling.

"We're rehearsing for Sunday. How do we sound?" From the delight on her face, I could tell she wasn't worried about it. "Are you hungry?"

"I love the music," I answered her first question. "Why don't you make a demo? I have a friend in the recording business. I'm sure he would be glad to help you with it. I can ask him if you like." Their music thrilled me as much as being in their company.

"To answer your other question," Nick said, slipping an arm around his mom. "Some supper would be nice. I've worked up an appetite." It must have seemed that all Nick cared about was food, but anyone seeing the way he looked at me would know better. I turned away, embarrassed, heading for the kitchen, but he came along. "Will you take a walk with me while Mom gets supper together?"

"I should help," I said. However, Bess dismissed that idea with a wave of her hand.

"We missed you over the weekend, especially my ole buddy here," Emilio said. I wondered whether Nick had kept our spontaneous tryst a secret. When Emilio picked Missy up, she glowed as if it were her birthday.

"I've never seen her having such a good time," I told them. "Thanks so much. I hope she wasn't in the way."

"She's a pure joy," Nick answered. "We all love her."

"I need to do some things around the house," I said again. I had taken enough advantage of Bess already, and besides, I was beginning to think I needed more time to sort out my feelings before I became too involved with Nick.

"Please?" Nick made me laugh with a happy clown face.

"Well, maybe."

"Hallelujah! She's going on a walk with me!" he shouted, making everyone smile. He was easy to understand because he didn't make a study of hiding his feelings.

Emilio excused himself saying he wanted to see his wife and kids. Nick went back to playing the upright while I set the kitchen table for supper.

Bess insisted we leave Missy with her so Nick and I took Zorba out into the late afternoon sunlight. When we got away from the house into what was called a prairie area Zorba quartered back and forth like a good retriever to see what he might stir up. In one fluid motion, Nick bent, picked up a stick, and hurled it into the air.

Zorba raced after it, reaching the spot where it fell seconds after it landed. He mouthed it, got it in a balanced grip, and continued down the trail ahead of us with head up, tail wagging jauntily.

When we left the prairie and entered the woods, I caught my breath at the sight of goldenrod blossoms, beautyberries, and bright red sumac backlit by the sun. After Nick helped me over a tree across the trail, he forgot to let go of my hand. I had to fall behind when the trail narrowed through low-growing bushes, but still he held on. Zorba's stick caught sideways on tree trunks as he tried to make his way down the trail, and since he could always find another one, Nick made him leave it.

"See the barbed wire and the remains of a post over there?" Nick pointed into the tangle of vegetation. "In the 1800s, the family raised cattle and grew oranges in this area."

Then he showed me a stand of palm fronds coming out of the ground. "These are saw palmettos," he said, fingering a big leaf with a dozen points on it. "Workers burned off the dead leaves and under-brush so that when the new palmettos sprouted, the cattle could eat them."

Nick continued. "That plant is still useful even though the cattle are long gone. Bees make honey from it, and Emilio gathers and sells wild berries to sell to food supplement manufacturers."

"What do they make from saw palmetto berries?" I asked. More and more I was becoming interested in natural alternatives to regular medical procedures.

"Um, well, prostate health," Nick mumbled.

"You mean they can treat some aspects of being male?" I hoped he could tell I was joking.

"Just couldn't resist that, could you?" His eyes crinkled with amusement, and I suddenly became wary. Was I flirting? I'd better be careful if I didn't want him to get the wrong idea...or the right one, which could be disastrous.

We moved into deep shade, where the small scrub oak trees wore patches of pink and white on their bark. Although I didn't think it was healthy for the trees, the pink was iridescent as the sun went down and beautiful.

"Is that pink some kind of algae?" I asked.

"It's called Thallophytic fungus." He stepped over and touched the tree. "It tells us the trees are old, but it won't attack anything else, so it's not a problem."

We continued to follow Zorba as he quartered ahead of us. He knew the way because he'd traversed the trail many times with his beloved master.

"This is an interesting part of the walk." Nick stopped when we emerged into an area where bushes had spread out over an acre or so. "It used to be a lakebed, and that makes the soil perfect for these wild blackberries. They're ripe now." He picked one, motioning for me to open my mouth.

As I savored the warm sweet fruit, he continued to teach. "Ordinarily," he said, "I leave them for the birds. They like wild elderberries too and they consume a many seeds of different kinds. You can tell if they're seedeaters by the shape of their beaks. Now look down," he said. I followed his gaze with my own.

"What am I looking for?" It would be a long time before I could see as he did. Maybe if Missy hung around him long enough, she'd grow up as full of knowledge of the land's secrets as Nick's cousin and my sister-in-law, Elaine, had. No, I mustn't think that way. Nick wasn't her father; Richard was. Then a thought hit me. If Richard were to take the role, she would learn what he knew. That didn't sound good to me.

"Take your time," he said as I crouched beside him, staring at a patch of sand, brown leaf particles, and twigs. I finally saw what I was looking for. There was a tiny moth so camouflaged with the patterns and colors of the sand and detritus, that you couldn't see the creature without scrutiny.

"How wonderful," I said, delighted. "It's a masterpiece of protective coloring."

"That makes it harder for birds and other animals to eat it," he said.

In this place and at this moment, I tasted pure happiness. Zorba, hot and panting after his exertions, rested up ahead.

"Good boy," the always gentle and soft-spoken Nick encouraged his dog. Why hadn't I met this kind of person before Richard trapped me? Or, a small voice said, before you trapped yourself. But then your beloved daughter would never have been born.

"Thanks for bringing me. I've had a good time on our walk," I told Nick. "Will we bring Missy sometime? You have a lot to teach us about nature and the woods." There I went, deepening our friendship almost unwittingly. The more I was with Nick, the less control I had over my emotions.

"I've got a problem," he said, holding his hand out to help me up a small rise.

My heart raced. It wasn't often you met a man who would talk about what was going on inside him. Maybe that was the reason he could periodically breach my fortresses. Hungry for that kind of intimacy, I waited.

"I intend to do something about the poaching and maiming of wild animals around here," he said as we topped the rise. "And I'm investigating drug smugglers who pass through this area," he said.

"But you're only responsible for the wildlife, aren't you?" I asked.

"Technically, yes, but my work and the sheriff's overlaps. I hate drugs. They ruin so many lives." He forgot he was holding my hand and squeezed hard. He let go when he felt me wince.

"I'm so sorry. Did I hurt you?" He looked stricken so I took his hand back to assure him I was all right and to keep him talking.

"They fly and ferry drugs up through the islands, at the tip of Florida, in single and double engine airplanes, speedboats, and fishing boats. We have vast areas of swamp, woods, and prairie and that makes it easy for them. From here, they smuggle them to New York City and points north. I'd like to short circuit the Florida part of the journey."

"That would be dangerous, wouldn't it?" I objected.

"I'm concerned about the animals too, especially the manatees," he went on, seemingly as glad for an audience as I was for him to talk to me.

"The speedboats the runners use are deadly for manatees that migrate into the St. Johns River and its spring fed tributaries during the cold months of the year. The propellers cut into the big mammals. I've never seen one dead or alive that didn't have scars. Other boaters do it too, but the drug runners are the worst. They don't care about anything except making money."

"I wish I could help." He whirled around and grabbed my shoulders.

"No! Those guys are deadly. Promise me you won't get mixed up with them!"

"What about the sheriff?" I hoped he didn't notice that I had promised nothing.

"They can't cover all that territory," he answered, letting go of me.

At the sound of a high-pitched "Keeoo," I looked up to see another hawk wheeling above the trees, and just then, Nick started walking so fast I could hardly keep up. When he stopped short. I ran into him. He cupped his ear to show he wanted me to hear something, so I closed my eyes and concentrated. When I did, I heard a series of flutters and squeaks that sounded like one of Missy's vintage pull toys.

Puzzled, I looked where he was pointing, then glanced at the dog, staring straight ahead without twitching a muscle.

"Quail," Nick whispered. "See?" I squinted, but again, could see nothing. As he moved close to explain, his touch made my whole body tingle. "The chicks are under the fallen leaves."

He smiled. "Their mother made a special noise, telling them to hide from the hawk, so they latched onto the leaves with their tiny claws and flipped over so they were hidden underneath."

I saw a leaf tremble and wondered at the miracle of nature. By now, my composure was gone. Being with Nick sent my emotions reeling in so many directions that sometimes all I could think of was just giving up and running away. Above all, I did not want him to know how close I was to throwing myself into his arms and begging him to hold me and love me forever.

CHAPTER 15

"This is where I found a dead sparrow hawk and two young ospreys." Nick prodded a cluster of weeds with his field boot.

"Why would people want to shoot that kind of birds when it's against the law?" I asked.

"We're not talking about law-abiding hunters. Those people actually do nature a service by judiciously culling the excess so the ones that are left will have enough to eat. We're talking about folks who think they should be allowed to do anything they want just because they want to," he said.

Surely, it all added up, but I had nothing concrete on which to base my suspicions. I decided to keep quiet until I could learn more.

"What is it?" he broke into my thoughts.

"Oh, nothing—we should get back; it's time for supper." We had walked in a big circle, so we were almost home.

"If you know something, even though I don't want you involved, I'd appreciate your telling me." Nick paused at the back door to kick the sand off his boots before we entered the kitchen. He then strode to the stove and lifted a pot lid from which steam escaped, making a chuckling sound.

"Turkey and noodles--and we've got mashed potatoes," Bess

announced with pride. How enticing it all smelled. Fresh air was a good appetizer. I would need to be careful about getting fat, but I had the feeling that if I gained a hundred pounds, these people would still love me. Ah, acceptance, the elixir of life.

"Noodles and potatoes make a lot of carbs for one meal." I'd remembered Mrs. McGregor's training.

"All part of our family inheritance," Bess said primly. Nick looked blank for a minute, then threw his head back and laughed. The resonance of his rich voice reached deep inside me, soothing my heart.

"She means heritage," Nick explained. "We don't know where the dish came from, but my sisters make it for their kids, too. It's inexpensive and filling. We probably got it from our less fortunate ancestors."

Bess smiled with a mother's tolerant patience, even though she didn't understand why he was laughing. This only son among daughters understood her and loved her, and that was all that mattered.

"Go sit and jaw a while," she said when supper was over. "Little sweetie and me can take care of these dishes. You got protection, Thaddeus?" I looked up, startled once again.

"Bug spray," he explained as red suffused his face. "We'll be okay, Mom."

"She shouldn't be stuck in the kitchen on a night like this; it's too beautiful out here," I whispered as we made our way to the front porch. "I ordered her a dishwasher."

"That's nice, but don't worry about her. She's happier than an otter on a mudslide just the way things are." He sat down on the swing as I sidled over to turn on the porch light. I was sorry when I started back to see that Zorba had climbed up, as big as he was, and now lay with his muzzle on Nick's knee.

The dog groaned with pleasure as his master massaged his ears, but then Nick gently pushed at Zorba and the dog exited the swing.

From Bess's kitchen radio came the plaintive "It Don't' Hurt Any More," sung by Grand Ole Oprey star, Hank Snow. Suddenly, I realized the song applied to my present feelings about Richard. Truly, he couldn't hurt me any more. Hank looked at me as I sighed with relief.

"What are you thinking about?" He settled back, cocking his head in a listening gesture.

"Those old songs get under my skin," I explained. "Some opera pieces do too, in a different way." I shrugged to show I took the subject lightly, but he wasn't fooled.

"You like highbrow stuff because you're a fine lady. I'm more of a hick, so I like country music better," he said, leading me on.

"Look at that moon." I verbally danced him away from starting a discussion about feelings. "It's a balloon hiding behind a lacy cloud."

"It's a beauty, all right." He pinned me with his gaze, obviously wanting to say more.

"Harvest moon." I shivered and wrapped my arms around myself. A new song had started: "I Love You Because," and I began to sing along almost under my breath. With a total lack of self-consciousness, his deep voice joined my lighter one and we followed each other through without embarrassment, in perfect harmony.

"I love you because you understand, dear every single thing I try to do. You're always there to lend a helping hand, dear, I love you most of all because you're you." When the song ended, I saw two tears splash onto the boards at his feet.

"What is it?" I asked, taken unaware. "Are you all right? Well, obviously you're not all right, but what can I do?" His body shook, making the swing quake. I reached out, but light caught the fire in my opal ring and flashed a stop signal. Touching right now would be too intimate. I pulled back.

"It's good to cry," I said in an attempt to comfort him. My statement was so shallow I expected him to get up and walk away, but he didn't. Suddenly I saw him as a small boy in ragged overalls with no shirt or shoes, standing with his fists clenched, trying to *be a man* and keep the tears away.

"Just sit here with me," he said, quietly clearing his throat while I sat gripping the swing chain until my fingers hurt.

"There's something no one knows," he said, but before he could explain, Bess appeared in her rolled-up jeans and long-tailed shirt with a dishtowel over her shoulder. I could have screamed with frustration!

"I'm so glad Nick has somebody nice to talk to," Bess commented, unaware that she had interrupted anything. Nick quickly pressed the heels of his hands against his cheekbones, but she didn't seem to notice.

"Is it okay if Missy calls me 'Grandma Bess'?" She waited for my nod and continued. "All my grandchildren call me that."

"Her grandkids love her." He sounded hoarse, but he was including his mother in the conversation.

She slid into one of the wicker chairs I'd brought down from the attic. "Poor boy, he's had such a hard time since his Constance died—and the baby." All the sadness of the ages was in her voice.

"When the end of life comes, there's nothing left but love and family and maybe a few friends. Them what don't have it are the ones who'll wish for it most. No offense, but money and beauty don't hold a candle to real, deep fondness, and not just for children, but between married lovers, too." As his mother talked, I sensed him watching me. I considered Bess's words and nodded.

"But friendship is easier," I interjected, wishing I could live in a world of contentment instead of being buffeted by the winds of romance.

"Married folks can make a group with God that works better than anything."

Where could she be headed with such a statement? I had only a second to wait until her index fingers and thumbs formed a triangle.

"You got God at the top point, the husband at one bottom point, and his wife at the other." She smiled and wiggled the triangle. "That way God leads and everybody asks him how to act, and then they can agree on things most of the time. God has the keys to life; if you don't have him, you don't have nothing." She looked at Nick for affirmation.

"Mom, you're right," Nick said, obliging her.

"That's what loving is all about--getting along, making God happy, letting him show you how to make each other happy. Nobody understands it, least of all me, but something mysterious happens at a wedding ceremony. You can't get the same thing by living together."

"I've never heard it put like that, but it makes sense," I said, willing to be as honest as I could about my situation. "My way got me a daughter for whom I am deeply grateful, but the down side was a lot of guilt and confusion."

"Honey, you had your troubles, but there's forgiveness and a new life. That's what I told my kids whenever they did something that bothered their conscience. 'Wait till you're married if you want the best

God has for you, and marry the right person. Let the Holy Spirit sing through you when you're together.'"

She folded her hands over her stomach, and looked up at the stars. "That's how it was with me and Nick's daddy. Thaddeus is a love child, for sure." She patted Nick's knee, and I knew without even looking that he had to be grinning.

CHAPTER 16

"My boy coulda been a star if he was a mind to. His daddy taught him guitar, and I taught him piano. He picked it up real quick. He takes the wildlife awful serious, though--doesn't have time for music much." Bess babbled away, unmindful of interrupting anything more than an after-dinner chat. Nick sat looking at the floor.

"Your whole family cares about the environment," I replied. "Without Elaine, my brother would still be bulldozing trees." I was only playing at politeness. Why didn't she go away so Nick and I could talk?

"Is Hank excited about the coming event?" Bess had a look of anticipation on her face. She'd love that child and nurture it, even though it was only a shirttail relative. How I wished she were Missy's real grandmother. I also wished my parents had lived long enough for their grandchildren to know them.

"Hank can hardly wait." I came out of my inward thoughts to answer her.

"Six o'clock comes mighty early," Bess said at last, and Nick hurried to help her rise.

"It will be easier when you move in here," I said to soothe her.

"Early is the best part of the day," she retorted. "Give me a hug before I go." I got up and she enveloped me in her soft arms. Nick got a quick hug too, and then Bess was gone. The minute I got out of the way, Zorba jumped back onto the swing. Anxious to get my place back, I stood over the dog until he flopped to the floor. My nearness seemed to encourage Nick to resume his tale.

"I never could understand why Constance married me. Within a year, I found out she was seeing her old boyfriend." He shrugged, stood up, and began to pace. "She was a real looker, I'll tell you that!"

"That doesn't mean she could do anything she wanted," I said.

"I was young and ignorant about girls. Basketball, music, and the woods were all I cared about. She was such a waif, though, with a bad home life, that I must have wanted to rescue her. I didn't know then that she was already pregnant and playing me for a fool." Nick seemed lost in thought as he returned and sat heavily on the swing.

"She didn't love you?" I wanted with all my heart to comfort him.

"No, but still, I would have been a good father," he murmured. "It wasn't the child's fault Constance was deceptive."

He put his arm around me, and went on talking. "One night when I was on gator duty, she went out with her boyfriend and they had a car accident. Constance and the baby were both killed. The guy survived. At first, I wanted to kill him; I knew I could get away with it. However, I'm not the type, so instead of taking action, I took up a grievance, which of course, made me depressed.

"I went to an old cabin in the swamp for a while. Eventually, I started yelling at God. It didn't seem to bother him any, though, and I realized it was futile. He was God and I was a mere human being with no power of any kind. Then peace started flowing in and I began to reason with him and try to negotiate a better, wiser life for myself.

"I gave up my grievance and the world began to shine and sparkle again. It's been a tough four years, but finding you--sharing this trust..."

Aching, I reached up to stroke his cheek. As if we were partners in a slow *pas de deux*, he pulled me to him. We looked deeply into each other's eyes. He kissed me, long and deeply, the heat of his lips surprising me with joy that poured through my being. I came to my senses and, terrified, tried to back off.

"Shh, it's all right," he said in a husky whisper when I tried to pull away. He loosened his hold, but kept me close. "What do you *really* want out of life, Jean?" he whispered.

"What do you want?" I asked as if his desires could give direction to mine. I rested my head on his chest as if everything I ever needed was contained within the circle of his arms. His heart beat steadily and I thought mine followed its rhythm.

"I know what *I* want!" he said. I could feel him smiling in the dark. "Did you ever wonder if your confusion might be saying you don't really like the idea of spending the rest of your life with Richard?" His low voice vibrated against my ear.

"I admire your commitment to morality, but, you know, God's thoughts are not the same as our thoughts. Maybe instead of assuming you know what he wants, you could ask him."

"Are you saying that I'm not a bad girl? Because I did give myself to someone I wasn't married to."

"Please don't beat up on yourself any more. You're an excellent person in every way." He kissed my forehead, gave my shoulder a squeeze, and glanced down at his watch.

"We definitely need to continue this conversation, but it's time for me to leave. I'm on gator duty again tonight so I'll take Zorba with me. Poachers are wily at night when they suspect somebody's around, but you can't outwit a good dog when it comes to hearing the smallest noises and smelling one molecule in a million that doesn't fit in. Come on, buddy, its' time for work." He slapped his thigh and Zorba got up, wagging his tail.

When they left, I felt restless. First, I went upstairs and stood watching over Missy. Five minutes later, I descended to the kitchen, hoping to find a task to complete, but Bess had been thorough and the kitchen gleamed.

I wandered into the parlor and stared at the stacks of dusty boxes, but they held no appeal. Once again, I climbed the stairs, and Violet's trunk caught my eye.

The first thing my hand fell on was a silk nightgown tucked and trimmed with ribbon and lace. When I lifted it out and held it up to myself, I realized Violet must have been about my size.

A taffeta slip followed and a foundation garment that would give shape to a dress. They called them 'girdles.' I took off my shorts and shirt and put the two last items on, then found a soft georgette dress with a softly draped collar to wear.

The fabric was so thin it slid easily through my circled thumb and finger. Nowadays, it would make a delightful wedding dress…if I could ever bring myself to marry…anyone. I whirled into my room — fantasizing that I was Ginger Rogers from the old movies dancing with Fred Astaire. Standing in front of the full-length mirror, I actually felt good about my looks for the first time in a long time. All I needed was the right hair-do and I'd be spectacular.

At the sound of a creaking stair, I tiptoed onto the landing, preparing to go downstairs and investigate in the now-eerie silence. But without warning, rough hands reached out and grabbed me.

"You ought to lock your doors, babe. You look delicious enough to eat."

It was Richard!

In a purely reflexive action, I panicked and shoved at him with all my might. The next thing I knew, he was tumbling down the stairs with his head banging on every step. I didn't mean to hurt him, just make him leave me alone.

Knowing he had to be dead, I flew down the stairs, feeling as if I were in the middle of a nightmare. I knelt beside him where he lay sprawled on the floor and checked his pulse. Right then, his arms came around me and I was trapped.

"That wasn't nice, babe, but I've got you now!" He flipped me on my back and tried to kiss me, but on the verge of nausea, I moved my head out of the way.

"Come on, you're no fun anymore, Jean!" He jumped up, towering over me. "You're nothing but an old maid mother."

"Shut up, Richard!" I rose quickly and stood as stiff and strong as a warrior. He took a step back in surprise.

"Okay, babe," he said, grinning at my boldness. "You haven't been over to see my place, yet," he began. "You promised to come."

"All right," I said, letting my shoulders relax.

"Well, okay, if you'll come tomorrow, I'll leave you alone for now. But you better get your act together. I've got my rights."

He turned and stalked out, rubbing the back of his head, leaving me shaking with fury and wondering what "rights" he thought he had in my life or in Missy's. Then a scary thought came...could he be considering DNA testing? Would he try to take her away from me? No, chance---was there?

CHAPTER 17

The next day, winter decided to make an appearance and I had a big decision to make. I didn't like being cold, but I thought Richard would be waiting for me and I didn't want to risk him coming to Living Spring. I put on a pair of cords and a Pendleton shirt and headed for the estate.

The defroster cleared the windshield, but made the air inside the car even colder. If I keep Mother's car, I thought, I'll need to get an overhaul to make sure everything works right. Maybe I'll get a new one, though.

The overwhelming grief and its accompanying melancholy I'd felt at my parents' death had begun to take a back seat to the new life Missy and I were beginning to experience. Nick would go shopping with me; he probably knew a lot about cars.

Richard had given me directions and as I turned onto a private drive, Raker, of all people, stepped out from a small guardhouse. His longish hair brushed the collar of the army camouflage jacket he wore with his jeans.

"Hello, beautiful lady," his voice rang out as I pressed the button to lower the window. I almost put it up again as waves of bad breath assaulted my senses. I made up my mind right then to talk to Hank about making Raker an appointment with a dentist.

"Where does Richard live, please?" I grabbed a tissue from my purse and patted my nose.

"I bet he's not expecting *you*." The man grinned, exposing what rotting teeth he had left.

"He asked me to come." I pressed the accelerator, revving the motor to indicate I didn't intend to sit there all day.

"Go on up the drive and around that curve. He lives over the garage. Too bad he don't believe in sharing his overflow." The man was actually leering, but I had no idea what he was talking about.

Fog muffled all sound as I went up the stairs and tapped lightly on the door. When I turned to survey the landscape below, I saw trees in a gray mist that made them seem to float. After what seemed a long time, Richard answered the door wearing a yellow tank top and a pair of red shorts that flared around thighs as thick as young trees. His hair hung halfway down his back. Suddenly I hated it, and him.

"I didn't think you'd really come. Wait here a minute." As he closed the door in my face, the fog continued to soak into my light wrap and I wished with all my heart I was at Living Spring sharing a cup of coffee, and yes, maybe even a pastry with Bess in her warm kitchen.

The door opened again, and Richard stepped aside for me to enter a tiny, filthy galley.

"Is this a bad time?" I asked. Now that I was in, I'd just as soon get the visit over with as quickly as possible.

"No, you can talk to me while I shave."

The stubble on his chin rasped as he ran his hand over it. His bloodshot eyes blinked as if even this dull morning was too bright for him. We proceeded into a large bed/sitting room that could have been a set for a film noir.

Black carpet and stark white walls made it seem even colder than it was, but if he would make the bed, remove the beer cans, empty the overflowing ashtrays, and pick up the newspapers, it would at least be acceptable. I hated breathing the stale air that reeked of cigarettes and beer. If only he would open a window—but of all things, he had the air-conditioner going full blast. He switched on the stereo and heavy metal music assaulted my ears.

"Sorry my bed's not made!" he yelled. "I know you always make

yours before you get out of it." He threw the sheet up over the rumpled sheets as he spoke.

"I do not! I just like to put things right…" I tried to shout over the cacophony, but it was no use so I started to empty an ashtray into a newspaper. He grabbed it and rolled it up, but not before I saw red stains on some of the cigarette butts.

"Was that lipstick?" I pulled my jacket closer around me.

"What? Are you crazy? Whose would it be?" He stuffed the paper into a nearby wastepaper basket.

While he wasn't looking, I opened another door that came off the room and led into a hallway. Out there, I could smell drugstore cologne, but it wasn't worth it to accuse him, so I shrugged and kept my own counsel. If we started fighting, it could take hours, and be nothing but sound and fury, because I was getting a strong feeling that we would never agree on anything. I followed him into the small bathroom so he could shave, and I sat on the closed toilet seat while he smoothed on shaving cream.

"Here, you do this for me." He handed me a straight razor.

"Why don't you use an electric shaver?" I asked, arranging the razor properly in my hand.

"This is so much more elegant," he said changing places so I was standing and he was sitting. I may as well take advantage of having you here," he smirked.

How do you know I won't cut your throat?" I said, shocking myself.

"I'm not afraid of you. You don't have the guts to do anything like that." He turned his cheek up toward the blade. "Get going. I want to show you something."

I ran the blade down his cheek, collecting shaving cream and washing it under the faucet as I went and had him shaved in no time.

He caressed his face. "Ah, Jean, no one can put a shave on a man like you can."

"I suppose many have tried." Anger was building, but I tamped it down.

"Do you like this shaving lotion?" He stuck an open bottle under my nose, and I sneezed. "No? Try that," he said. The second one wasn't wonderful, but at least I didn't seem to be allergic to it.

"What the…" Richard had just wiped his hands on a towel when we heard a noise in the next room and I looked out to see Raker with a small blonde who wasn't any older than seventeen or eighteen. The bits of jewelry on the lapels of her jean jacket were tarnished.

"And who would this be?" I asked Richard, lifting an eyebrow. Everyone ignored me and looked at Richard.

"Oh, for Pete's sake," he said.

"Out here." She opened the door to the hallway, and Richard followed her, but left the door open.

I sat down on the unmade bed, not knowing what else to do with myself, and Raker sank down beside me. At least he had washed and changed his shirt and he smelled better, until he opened his mouth. He held out a cigarette, which I declined. For the first time in my life, I was grateful for the smell of cigarette smoke because it masked his breath somewhat.

"Looks like you two were about to get it on," he said. "Sorry we busted it up." I hated the lax expression on his face, but thought I might try a soft answer and see where that got me.

"Believe me, I wasn't having fun," I said. Raker and I sat a comfortable distance apart, watching Richard and the girl.

"Did he hurt you?" The ferret-like face looked anxious as I shook my head.

"I can't hear what she's saying because of the music." I said, getting up to turn it off.

"That's Trixie. He said he'd go away with her before the boss came back, but she just found out the boss will be in this afternoon," Raker replied. "Look at that! Richard don't like it when she puts her fists on her hips thataway."

As we watched, Richard shoved at the girl's hands, but suddenly she slapped him. Raker gave a low whistle as we watched Richard grip her shoulders and shake her like a terrier killing a rat. I started to get up, but he stopped before I could make a move.

I turned to Raker and asked quietly, "How did he think he was going to take her away somewhere and yet stay here with me all at the same time?"

"He made them promises before he seen you again." Raker

shrugged. "I bet he's telling her the deal's off. You can see she don't like it." He grinned his ugly grin.

The door slammed back against the wall, followed by Trixie who, propelled by Richard's racquet arm, stumbled across the room and landed in our laps.

"Take her back to the big house," Richard said, looming over us all. "I can't do anything because of all the stupid women around here. Why'd you bring her out here, anyway?"

He reached down and gave Raker a cuff on the ear. Raker put his hand up to it and looked at me for sympathy. I gave him not a blink.

"We'll get you for this," Trixie hissed, getting to her feet. "I've got friends, and you know them too."

"Come on, Raker." She stalked out, and Raker, in his wrinkled shirt, turned back to shrug and raise his eyebrows as if to say there's no telling what she might do next. I rushed after them, not waiting to stay in the company of whatever demons Richard might unleash now.

CHAPTER 18

"Hey, babe, where you going?" Richard grabbed my arm and whipped me around. I was so angry I almost hit him, but I knew that wouldn't be smart. He could easily hurt me permanently in some way.

"It looks like I'm just a third wheel here right now." I reasoned, taking a deep steadying breath.

"Ah, come on; give me a chance to explain," he said, false charm oozing like cream from a carton. "That little piece was nothing. Besides, I still haven't shown you what I wanted to—now that you're here…" He tugged on my sleeve, and I felt my resistance lessen. It might be a good idea to get all this over and then perhaps we could each go our own way.

"All right, but it better be good." Hmm, yes, I thought, maybe I would eventually learn something that would help somebody.

Downstairs, we walked out on a long pier that jutted into a lake. He opened the door of the most luxurious boathouse I'd ever seen and invited me to take a seat beside him in the speedboat it contained. He stroked the polished teak.

"After we get the airplane, me and you will own a beauty like this. Don't worry; I'll save you some money on the plane. All I need is a used single engine Cub."

He got out of the boat and I followed, wondering what he was talking about. We approached an airboat sitting in the open. He settled me on a bench seat and gave me ear-protectors. He then perched in the rear close to the propeller cage, which roared to life at a touch.

The sound was so shattering that my whole body went into spasms for a moment. When I regained my senses, I quickly positioned the ear protectors; even though I was certain they made me look like a bulbous-eyed dragonfly.

As we skimmed the lake, I began to enjoy the ride, and suddenly Nick's voice came to me. "I'd like to take you out in the airboat, Jean." He had described how such a vessel passed over saw grass as if it weren't there. Oh, why wasn't I with him instead of Richard? I could trust Nick with my life, not so with Richard.

It took all my strength to hang on as g-forces pressed me against the back of the seat and an icy rain began to sling needles at my face. We went into a long curve that fetched us into the St. Johns River heading upstream and from there into another run. I didn't know whether to laugh with exhilaration or scream in terror as we careered through channels, barely missing hummocks and cypress knees, one after another.

It seemed Richard was over-confident and careless, but it didn't occur to me then that he simply might not be as proficient as he thought he was. We eventually approached an island where the shake-shingle roof of a house peeked through trees. I looked where we were going and I saw a pier upon which sat a large gas pump. I was afraid, suddenly, that we were going to hit it and be blown to smithereens, but we slowed and drifted to safe harbor.

I thanked God, but as I struggled up, my body trembled with exhaustion, tension, and cold. A lull revealed no other sound except wind sighing through the pines.

"You wouldn't believe how bored the women are with this place." Richard said, tying down the frisky craft. "They come out with rich old duffers to *keep them company*," he said, laughing. "Dumb broads. Don't worry, though, babe, I'd get beat up *and* lose my job if I messed around with any of those bimbos."

A good-sized lodge with bushes growing around the foundation rose into sight as we went up an incline. We climbed the steps to the porch and I looked around at hanging planters filled with dead plants. The house was chilly inside, but the Early American maple furniture made the living room look cozy.

"I get sick of trying to keep things up," Richard said, heading for the fireplace where he threw in wood from a pile nearby. I remained silent for once. "I may be a glorified janitor-chauffeur now, but when we go into business together, I'll be my own man."

"What business?" I pulled a cushioned rocking chair with maple armrests closer to the fire.

"We can talk about that later." He tweaked the thermostat. First, there was a blast of cold air and then the heat started to flow around me.

"That feels good." I held my hands close to the young flames licking the kindling to life. The sudden warmth made me sleepy and languorous.

"Why don't you get out of those wet clothes," he suggested. I couldn't resist the idea of further warmth and dryness. I looked around. "Over there." He nodded toward the hallway leading off the main room. "You'll find something to wear in the first bedroom. The chicks are always leaving their junk behind."

Soft classical music began to flow from cleverly concealed speakers in the ceiling. The builder had hidden all modern devices to retain the illusion of a rustic cabin. I found a pair of jeans and a hand knitted Irish fisherman's sweater hanging in the closet. Both were too big and the musty smell blended with somebody else's strong perfume, but at least they were dry. I knew my sense of smell would soon adjust. I braided my hair and returned to my host.

"Okay, now come with me." He led me outside and down the steps of a wooden deck.

After we walked for some distance, we began hearing peeping sounds that seemed to float on the heavy air. I'd heard the sounds before, but I couldn't quite place them. The path rounded a bend, and there in front of us was a sprawling wire pen enclosing an enormous coop that Richard had to stoop to enter. Inside were hundreds of quail in various stages of maturity. They strutted and pecked. Some sat in egg boxes. My gaze sought Richard's, inviting him to explain.

"The big boss buys goodwill from his international associates with quail hunts and dinners out of doors. We serve some great food: quail they shoot themselves, minus birdshot, of course, caviar, salmon, lobster, and plenty of booze. The boss provides German shotguns." He rubbed his fingers together to indicate money. "You wouldn't believe how those rich guys keep trying to make off with them when they leave.

"I'm in charge of hiring loaders and guides. My men scare the birds up so the rich guys can shoot them. You want a rush; you should be here when the birds all rattle skyward and the guns start firing as if it was and shoot out on Main Street. Me and Raker make good money. We were going to save up for a single engine Cessna together, but I came up with the idea of letting you in on it. That way it won't take so long to get the enterprise up and running."

"If you intend to smuggle drugs into the country in an airplane, you're crazy to think I'd have anything to do with it." My counselor would applaud my signs of emotional and mental growth: long gone was the time when I'd swallow anything Richard said without questioning it.

"Me, drugs?" Richard pointed at himself and laughed. "How could you think such a thing of me? Who have you been talking to?"

"I don't understand." I shook my head. "Did you say you wanted to marry me?" He nodded. "Is the only reason because I have money and you want it?"

"Come on now, you know I love you, babe," he whined. "I swear to God …" I stepped away from him and almost fell over a bird that was underfoot. "We need the plane fairly soon because this is our chance to get in the loop."

Realizing I'd need to tell Nick all about this, I began to feel like the famous World War II spy, Mata Hari.

"Does shooting hawks and ospreys have anything to do with these quail?" I asked.

"Not really. We just like to have a bit of sport ourselves and they're more exciting to shoot," he said.

I could hardly believe he had admitted it! He and Raker had been killing raptors as casually as quail hunters killed quail, but quail wasn't on any endangered or even threatened list as far as I knew, and it wasn't illegal to shoot them, though it might be illegal to breed them without a permit. I'd have to leave the sorting out to Nick and Emilio, but it sounded as if, when they made a bust, it could put some bad people out of commission for a while.

Could I tell Nick all this or would my customary loyalty toward Richard stop me? From here on, I'd have to be careful not to antagonize Richard. He might decide hurting one of us was going to help him in some way.

"Now if you want real sport," Richard said, "try shooting bald eagles. What a rush!" Richard rattled on, oblivious to my stare, and all at once, I saw how naïve I'd been. How could I have imagined I could ever learn to live with such a man?

"What kind of business is your boss really in?" I asked, probing further.

"Let's put it this way, he deals in a product that's much in demand in certain circles and on certain streets," Richard said.

"You mean he's a drug dealer?" I chewed at the fingernail on my index finger.

"That's a pretty crude way of putting it. Let's just say he meets some keenly felt needs," Richard said, laughing.

"And you plan to become one, too." The way he thought became more obvious the longer I knew him. My self-delusion dies hard, I thought. I had so wanted Missy's father to be honorable, and I wanted a real family for both of us more than anything in the world.

"Let's just say …" He sounded aggrieved. "I'm going to fly. I'll be in the air every day." He took my hand. "I'll do runs from south Florida to this area. We'll make so much money that Dad will have to acknowledge that I'm worth the mud chemicals I'm made of."

"What have I ever said or done to lead you to believe I would consider financing a drug running business? Don't you know me at all?" My heart was a heavy weight that had somehow fallen into the deepest part of me.

"Come on, babe, you're in business. You have your eye out for a good deal, or else, instead of tending to the money you already have, you'd spend all your time running around shopping and having lunch with the girls. Most people spend it before they even get it, but not you, I admire, you, babe! You wouldn't believe how much I admire you." His voice grew soft and he put his hands on my shoulders. I steeled myself to speak honestly to him, probably for the first time in our relationship.

"It's hard to describe how I feel right now. I loved you once and I thought that, because you were there for me when I needed someone, that you loved me too. However ..." I had a few things to say, but I wanted to say them in a way that wouldn't stir up his manly pride. "If we were really getting married, we'd have many things to work out. We don't have the same principles, or care about the same things."

"You don't get it, do you? I'll marry you if you insist, because of your old-fashioned notions, but we don't have to be married to go into business together, or to make love." He tried to put his arm around me, but I moved carefully around the birds to elude him. "Oh, come on, don't be such a snob," he said. "Do you think your God cares what you do? I will tell you one thing. That God of yours has never done anything for me."

"If you would only take stock, you'd see. You have your health, and a beautiful little daughter. We could have had a good life if only... You brought me back from despair when my folks died. You were good to me. But I gave you more of myself than I should have."

With a mental shake, I determined to say what I really thought. "God gave me the courage to go ahead and have Missy. She's the greatest gift of my life; yours too, if only you could see it. Part of the reason I wanted to marry you was so she might know you as I did in those days."

"Listen, just marry me, buy me an airplane, and forget about all that." I'd never seen him truly desperate before. "You don't have to know what's going on in my day-to-day life. You can get on with raising your kid, fixing up your house, whatever you need to do. It'll be okay if you don't take an interest in my work. I'll be too busy to care anyway."

"Would you take me home, now?" I couldn't talk any more. He was breaking my heart, and it was obvious he would never hear what I was saying.

"Nothing has changed; you're still going to marry me?" he asked with a worried frown.

"We'll talk about it later." I knew I was on dangerous ground and sent up a silent prayer for help.

Richard got that cold, stubborn look on his face that always shut me out, and I knew he wasn't about to take me home yet. He started walking back toward the lodge. How many times did I have to end up in this kind of situation before I learned to avoid being with him in a setting from which I could not escape?

When we arrived back at the lodge, he got a beer out of the refrigerator and started drinking and talking crazy. I knew he would grow increasingly belligerent as he always did when in his cups. This could be the worst mistake yet. I needed to get home to Missy, Bess, Nick, and even Zorba, but how was I going to get off this island?

By late afternoon, he was drunk and I was in the middle of a full-fledged panic attack where my bones turned to jelly and I couldn't take a deep breath because of the tightness in my chest. I stopped answering as he grew ever more insistent that he would get his way no matter what I thought. Nothing I did or said was going to make any difference now. All reason had fled.

When darkness fell, I knew I'd have to make a few concessions, or he'd hold me captive all night. The werewolf in him would emerge as his consumption of alcohol increased.

"Okay, it's getting dark. Let's go," I demanded. "I'll think about what you've said."

Finally, something in his besotted brain shifted. He was egotistic enough to believe I would come around to what he wanted. We made our way to the airboat and started across the lake.

For a while, the broad beam of the headlights kept me hypnotized as we barely missed one island after another, but eventually I closed my eyes to escape the harrowing sight. How did he get away with such recklessness? I guess I shouldn't worry about it, I told myself, as long as we were on our way home, which at the moment, seemed a long way off.

CHAPTER 19

I pulled the car into the shed and walked to the house feeling exhausted, but the lively piano tune coming from the parlor put strength in me and I hurried to see Nick. Bess met me at the back door.

"Thank goodness, you're home," she said. "I was worried sick."

She called out, "She's home!" and Nick appeared in the doorway with Zorba.

Home! That word had never seemed so wonderful! This was truly my home and these people were my people. Zorba lay down at my feet and rolled onto his back so I would scratch his belly. I looked into Nick's face again and he looked back, smiling. I wanted to fall into his arms and sob, but instead I stooped down to the big dog.

"Hey, boy," I saw tears falling on him as he lolled, tongue hanging out and paws curled appealingly. I looked up at Nick, and he looking back, smiling.

"I'm sorry; I couldn't let you know where I was," I said, taking a deep breath.

"It's okay. I've been keeping an eye on the island, just got here, myself," Nick said. "I didn't want to intrude into your business. I left as it started getting dark, thinking to come back for you with reinforcements, if needed. I'm glad to see you made it out on your own."

"How was Missy?" I asked, feeling guilty for leaving her all day.

At some point, I'd tell Nick about day's progress into semi-madness, but this wasn't the time.

"She's had her bath and her story, and she's sound asleep," Bess answered. "Go take a peek; it will make you feel better." She was right. The sight of my beautiful daughter with her toss of red curls and her creamy skin comforted me.

"I love you and I'm going to protect you the best I can." I leaned down and kissed her on the forehead, and she said, "Mommy," in her sleep.

When Emilio got there, Bess invited him to stay and eat, but he'd been out every night that week on one call or another and wanted to go home and relax with the wife of his heart.

"Thanks for coming, ole buddy," Nick said.

"Oh, Miss Jean," Emilio said. "Let me give you my cell phone number in case you need me. Don't worry though; we're keeping an eye on those men."

"Come on and have some shepherd's pie, darlin'," said Bess when Emilio was gone. "Come on, Thaddeus, let's sit down and Jean can tell us all about her day."

"If she wants to," said Nick. After his warm greeting, he seemed to have cooled toward me, or was that just my imagination?

"I did something really foolish today. I knew better. I don't know why I did it," I told them.

"Did it have anything to do with Richard?" Nick asked, his smile now gone.

"Yes, it had everything to do with him." I unfolded the ironed and creased napkin and laid it across my lap.

Bess ladled a big spoonful of the shepherd's pie, which looked and smelled delicious, onto my plate, and my stomach growled its thanks. When Nick finished saying grace I took a deep breath and continued, "I told Richard I would visit him at his place to hear about a business proposition."

I forked a small bite of mashed potatoes off the top of the pile. It tasted wonderful. "Um, this is delicious, Bess. Thank you for having supper ready. Thank you, too, for taking such good care of Missy. She loves you and I know she had a good time with you." I dug down to the meat, peas, and carrots.

"Are you still on duty?" I asked Nick.

"No, I'm off tonight. Why?" he cocked his head and squinted at me. "Do you know something about the poaching?" He was so eager to hear what I had to say I couldn't help but tease just a bit.

"No, but I may know something about some other kind of poachers you'd be interested in."

"You two can talk about that after supper while I clean up," said Bess. "Right now, I want to tell you about some adorable things your little girl did and said today."

Bess started telling story after story of my wonderful child in such a lively way that I found myself laughing and almost crying. Nick seemed to enjoy the tales as much as I did, though no one, not even the kindest person can care about every pearl the way a mother, or even a pretend grandmother, can.

Nick and I moved languidly as we went into the parlor. He had worked all night the night before and stayed up all day today in case I needed him. He sat down on the piano bench with his back to the piano and I drew up the creaky office chair from close to Bess's bongo drum.

"Now I'm going to settle down and get the house done. We don't even have a decent place to sit and talk except the porch, and it's a bit too cool out there this evening," I said.

"I started looking for you at Elaine's," Nick said.

"I should have told someone where I was going. I'm sorry," I said. "Is she all right?"

"Seems she has been having a few labor twinges. It won't be long now," Nick informed me. "Now will you tell me what's going on?"

"I'm giving up on Richard," I said.

Nick sat up straight. "Good, Jean, I hate to say it about someone you once cared for, but he's rotten all the way through."

"I know that now." I said. "And, I know God can do anything in a person's life, but there's no sign that Richard wants change and I think wanting it, at least a little, has to be a prerequisite before God will move."

"What did he tell you?" Nick took a small notebook and the stub of a pencil from the breast pocket of his uniform. "Okay, go ahead. I'm taking notes for an official report."

"He was at the apartment…the mansion, actually. It's a mansion, isn't it?" I was trying to start my tale. He nodded. "I didn't see much of the house itself. Richard lives upstairs in a separate bed-sit. There were two other people around: Raker and a young girl who looked about seventeen or eighteen."

"He'd better hope she's eighteen," he said, then wrote in his notebook. I told him about the island, the cabin, and the quails.

Nick looked up from his notes and said, "I knew it was that bunch shooting the raptors. I wonder if his boss has permits to keep wild birds. He's breeding them, you say?"

I nodded. He looked full into my face and the smile was back. "The great thing about criminals is that they think they're above the law, but if you can't catch them for their big crimes, you can often get them on the misdemeanors. Once you start questioning, you run into every kind of dirt in the book, even the fact that most of them have no driver's licenses because they think they're above the law."

The next day, Bess moved in. She allowed me to help carry her few possessions and her clothes in from the car and then I went back to my seemingly endless task of sorting through boxes and the three of us settled in together more every day; really four, because anytime Nick was free, he was at the house.

When I finished the boxes, we started to organize cupboards and drawers all over the house. Annie had saved everything, as had her ancestors before her. We found, however, many objects of rare historical significance and a few collectors' items bought by someone when the grove and cattle businesses were thriving and they could afford some valuable trinkets and jewelry.

Every evening, when Nick brought Zorba over to guard us, Bess would say, "Thaddeus, are you staying?" We had such good times then.

He, Bess, and I told our life stories during the meal and afterwards Nick played the piano and taught me some of the old country hymns such as "Down to the River to Pray."

He said I had a great singing voice and asked me to stand up front

Sunday with the praise team and help lead. Our choir and symphony at the big church in town had been comprised mostly of people with long musical experience and education, so I hadn't really known I could sing, but I knew many songs just from being in the congregation. Here my voice fit into the melody while Bess, who could sing anything, took the alto part. We began practicing with Emilio in the evenings.

The house seemed even more crowded since we'd brought everything down from the attic and out of the drawers and cupboards for the auction. The auctioneer's staff would have done the work, but we wanted to see and touch things that older family members had deemed valuable, and to give the family members a chance to keep anything they wanted.

Strangely, for women who had come from a family of keepers, Bess, Annie, and Elaine selected few items. They were rejoicing that the house would soon be beautiful again, and a real home and they were loath to clutter the spaces they lived in now that they had moved away from it.

One night after we practiced our songs for Sunday, Nick said he and Emilio wanted to open up the fireplace in the parlor. I was looking forward to seeing where this mysterious fireplace was.

As I suspected, it was the place where the wall came forward between the two windows. When they began slamming the wall with big rubber mallets, I was dismayed. Nick handed me one and encouraged me to swing it with all my might, which I did. I started yelling every time I hit it. The others tried to shush me so I wouldn't wake Missy, but it felt so good to have the inner struggle begin to seep away with every stroke that I couldn't stop.

In a few minutes, the brick fireplace was exposed and I knew we had discovered another treasure. The aged handmade bricks came in beautiful earth tones: reds, yellows, browns, and blacks. Nick said he knew exactly where the granite mantelpiece was and would bring it in and install it for us.

The next day I called a fireplace man to clean the chimney and make sure that everything would work properly and safely for a good long time.

My friend from the antique store sent an auctioneer for a preliminary visit one evening and it was old home week because he knew Emilio and Nick from law enforcement auctions of confiscated cars, boats, and planes. They had a good time talking about some of the odd things they found over the years, such as a small shark one crime boss kept in a giant aquarium in his indoor theater.

Because it was a matter of law to protect the wild creatures, Nick had to get permits to take it to Sea World where it would be safe and pampered for the rest of its sharkly life. I admired Nick's knowledge and patience. He had a sharp mind that I enjoyed tapping into at will.

At last, it was time for the auctioneer and his staff to appraise and price everything. The china for Elaine had gone to her house and she had paid Annie for it, plus appreciation, over the years. The sale would be partly in the yard and partly in the house. The staff could move everything indoors if it rained, but the weatherman gave us hope it would not.

The people in charge advertised on the Internet and in newspapers in all the surrounding states so we expected a big turnout. The Boy Scout master said if his guys could have a hot dog stand, they'd help with anything we needed. The historical society asked to come in Civil War costumes and stage a battle so the auction turned into a community festival.

Nick invited our praise band to play and sing, but without amplification so we wouldn't blast people out of the yard with too much noise. The historical society brought costumes for all of us as well. Bess and I looked like ladies from *Gone with the Wind*, and Nick and Emilio wore Confederate uniforms. They looked so handsome I couldn't stop watching them.

I noticed when they stood still for any length of time their legs were far apart as if they'd been trained to stand that way so no one could push them over or unbalance them. It was a grand day and the most fun I ever had in my life.

It turned out to be a beautiful day with low humidity and a sweet breeze to cool us. Mrs. McGregor came with Hank and Elaine and they looked after Missy, who thoroughly enjoyed the children's carnival and the bouncy castle.

I couldn't imagine why Richard didn't show up, but was deeply thankful that he hadn't. I made plans to share the bulk of the proceeds with Annie, because after all, everything had belonged to her ancestors, not mine. I hoped it would help make her and Ira more comfortable and more able to enjoy some alternative health care providers that insurance wouldn't pay for.

CHAPTER 20

One day, Bess left to visit her daughter in Oviedo, and that night Missy and I were alone because Nick had duty and needed Zorba. I took Missy upstairs to bed and remembered halfway up the stairs that I hadn't checked the locks yet. I would do that as soon as she went to sleep.

As I was coming back downstairs, I heard the kitchen door slam and ran to see who it was. Maybe Nick was coming back for something.

But, no. It was Richard. "Where's the kid," he demanded as he proceeded to throw himself into a chair, letting his long legs stretch into the kitchen.

I detected an all too familiar slur in his voice and smelled the marijuana on his clothes. It brought back a combination of emotions: a mixture of fear and terrible memories of the days when he called it "recreational."

"She's in bed asleep," I said, silently berating myself for not locking the doors. "And I want you out of here."

"Get her up, and don't take that tone with me or you'll be sorry." He glared and a shot of adrenaline hit my brain, bringing all my senses to life.

I'd have to be crafty this time. No more self-examining, yet self-defeating honesty. It just didn't work, as he could turn on me without warning. I clasped my hands together to stop their shaking, and the next thing I knew they were moving, wringing, as though I was rubbing in hand cream without having been conscious of it. I took a deep breath and held it for a count of seven, determined to ward off panic.

"Move it!" He slammed his fist on the tabletop, making the salt and peppers jump.

"Let's not disturb her," I wheedled. "She'll be cranky, and you won't like that." I looked around for some kind of answer, or an escape, or a weapon, but there was nothing.

"Never mind I'll get her myself. Which room's she in?" He rose and stalked to the stairway. I hurried after him, trying to catch hold of his shirt, but he was moving too fast.

"No, please don't. You can come back and see her in the morning." I caught the shirt, but he wrenched away and kept going.

"In here?" He threw open a door with such force that it banged against the wall of Bess's vacant room. He kicked the second one open, but when he saw that it too was without an occupant, he turned around and grabbed my hair, pulling my head back and throwing me off balance.

It hurt so much it brought tears to my eyes. With all my heart, I wished I had taken a self-defense class. If I had, I'd throw him down the stairs, and this time it would be on purpose.

"Let go of me," I managed to say.

He pulled my head so far back I had to fall to my knees. He swore and let go. But I couldn't get up in time to block him from finding the room in which Missy was sleeping. Besides, he was too big and I was too small in comparison. I wished I had taken self-defense classes the way Dad had wanted me to.

"Aha! There she is." He let out a cry of triumph as he headed for the sleeping child.

I ran in behind him, but he pushed me away and scooped her up. The bright moonlight coming in the window made them into a silhouette of father and child, which I had longed to see. But I knew I couldn't afford to be sentimental now; this was a time when I needed all my wits, but my anxiety was confusing me.

Missy snuggled against his chest as he brushed past and started downstairs, and I was glad that she was staying deep in slumber, as only the young and innocent could do.

"When you decide you want cooperate my way, you'll get her back," he said as he exited the back door.

"Please don't take her; I'll do whatever you want." I followed all the way to the car, weeping and begging; but he was deaf to my pleas, and I was no match for his muscular bulk. I changed tactics when I saw pleading would get me nothing.

"Wait, let me go too. Let me hold her." He opened the back door and slid her carelessly onto the seat. I clutched at the handle, but he jerked it out of my grip and slammed the door. He got in and started the motor, and left with me running alongside until I fell to the sandy road, sobbing in utter despair.

"Lord, help me," I prayed in desperation, lying there in the bright, cold moonlight. Suddenly, I seemed to receive an infusion of strength and determination.

I got up, straightened my shoulders, and returned to the house. I dressed in warm clothes and tried to call Nick, but reached only voice-mail. I called Emilio, too, but got voice mail. I called the sheriff's department, but the dispatcher began to tell me about the time her husband stole their child for a prank. I hung up on her.

Shuddering, I felt the fear Missy would experience when she woke up and found herself in a strange place with a man she clearly didn't like or trust. I prayed she wouldn't catch pneumonia from the cold night air. The least he could have done was to take a blanket.

I got a grinding sound from my mother's old car when I tried to start it. I vowed to get a new one at the first opportunity, one that would work in any situation. After another prayer for help with the car, it finally came to life, and I took off in pursuit.

Richard wasn't going to get away with it, I vowed. We'd see to it that he ended up behind bars for the rest of his life, Nick and I. How I wished someone would see me speeding on the way to the mansion where I was sure Richard had gone, someone who could help me get Missy back.

I soon reached the gatehouse to the estate. At this hour, I barreled right through the open gate as my mind cleared. I twisted off the headlights and ignition and coasted toward the light coming from the dock. Carefully and quietly, I steered behind one of the outbuildings, and crept from the car through the bushes to where I could see Richard and Raker carrying something like a rolled up carpet slung between them. Their loud voices carried on the night air.

"I popped him on the back of the head with his sap," came Raker's nasal twang. "They'll think he hit his head on something before he fell off the pier and drowned. I poured likker all over him so he'll smell bad." He laughed, pleased with himself.

My heart plummeted. For a moment, I stood petrified. Nick was in that roll and they planned to kill him. I prayed for an idea. Missy was probably still in the car; maybe she was still asleep. I faced what I had never allowed myself to face before; Richard and Raker were vicious criminals who actually enjoyed hurting things—and people.

"One, two, and three ..." Raker shouted and between them, they heaved the bundle into the water where it hit with a hollow splash. They started whooping and slapping their hands together, congratulating themselves. I crept closer as they headed for Raker's car.

"We got time for a couple before we take off," Richard said. I crept down to the water and soon heard rock music coming from the car radio.

~

As they started for the dock, probably to get the airboat. I ran bent over through the shadows, all the while thanking God for my lifeguard training. Nick was in the most danger right now.

Out of the corner of my eye, I saw Richard take Missy out of the car, still asleep. I could hardly believe she was sleeping through all of this. He took her to the boathouse and I felt she was safe for the moment because Richard's plan was more to get money than to hurt our little daughter.

When they went back to the car, I ran down to the lake's edge where the rolled up carpet laid half in and half out of the water where they had tossed it as if it were a bag of garbage. I was furious, but grateful the two of them had drunk enough to be careless. I waded in and began to tug and pull on the soggy bundle until I got it onto the beach, then I crouched and pushed at it to make it unroll. At the last push, there was Nick! He moaned softly as I knelt beside him, the grandest and most glorious gift I had ever unwrapped.

"Nick," I whispered, stroking his cheek. He blinked and opened his eyes, alive and awake, but not focusing yet.

"J-Jean?" he said weakly. I laid my hand over his mouth, even though I knew Raker and Richard wouldn't be able to hear anything over the radio. I presumed they'd gone back to the car for one more beer before they did anything else, and counted on the time to revive Nick and see if we could find a way to foil them.

"Shh, it's all right. I'm here," I whispered.

"My dear, love." Nick sounded disoriented, but he was coming around in spite of Raker's bashing. My spirits soared. Suddenly he put his arms around me and drew me down for a slow, sweet kiss on my quivering lips. Even though I didn't have time for it, still, for a split second, I forgot that we were in the middle of an emergency.

"Will you marry me?" His vague, love-filled eyes gazed into mine. I felt a confirmation of rightness and nodded as I helped him sit up.

"Raker hit you," I said. "He and Richard rolled you in this rug and were planning to drown you."

He nodded with slowly returning awareness and rolled over on his hands and knees so he could get up. He gazed at the soggy carpet upon which he sat. A frown creased his forehead, and even though I was in a hurry, I knew I would need to slow down and give him some details before we could figure out what to do.

"Wouldn't it be kind of strange for me to 'accidentally' drown, rolled up in a rug?" He gave a snort of laughter.

Here was the quick, bright Nick I knew and loved, the one who could find humor in the worst of circumstances.

"They must have come up behind me when I was getting out of the truck. "Where's Zorba? I was just going around to let him out ... they left him shut up. I can't believe I let them sneak up on me."

"They're drunk," I explained, "and on drugs. Nothing they're doing makes any sense. If you feel okay now, we have to get Missy away from them."

"Dear God, don't tell me those two have Missy?" Nick got up and kicked at the rug. "Let's get going!" He gave my hand a hard squeeze as if he could hardly contain the excitement of the chase and I knew he'd be all right.

The car radio silenced. I heard Missy crying, working up to a screaming fit that I knew could be formidable. We could see the two men, the shorter one carrying her, setting off for the boathouse, and I prayed they wouldn't notice us.

"Go easy now, but hurry," Nick said. We followed them, but were too late to stop them before they started the engine of the speedboat and roared off in the direction of the St. Johns River.

"This way," I said, tugging on his hand. "There's an airboat at the end of the pier." We ran hand in hand down the beach and without hesitation, Nick jumped in and started the machine as I got myself onto the bench seat in front.

"They'll be going to the lodge," I yelled at the top of my lungs.

Nick nodded, handing me the ear protectors and the boat shot forward. In no time, we were up the river and into the swamp, weaving around islands and skimming over saw grass. The speedboat made bad time because it wasn't as versatile as the flying boat. I was terrified for Missy, though, because the others were going too fast and zigzagging as if out of control.

Please dear God, please protect my little girl, I prayed. Suddenly, I saw the speedboat curve sharply as a bulky figure catapulted from its side and into the water. I didn't know who had gone overboard, but I hoped that whoever it was had taken Missy with him.

As we approached the spot, I hollered at Nick to slow down and when he did, I chose an open span of water and jumped in too. Remembering Missy had a course when she was two that taught her to swim as a reflex whenever she hit the water eased my fears some-what. Yep, there she was, a tiny figure in the vast swamp treading water.

"Hi, Mommy," she said calmly. "Are you going to save me?"

I was so proud of her and so grateful to God for keeping her safe and calm that tears began to run down my face in what seemed like cascades. I dunked my head under the freezing cold water to clear them and came up to touch Missy and reassure myself that she was real and that she was all right. I knew that I should leave her on her own as long as she was doing so well treading water because it was keeping her circulation going, but I stayed close enough to support her if she should tire.

We waited for Nick to circle slowly back around to pick us up. Suddenly a great explosion turned the sky ablaze and I knew the speedboat had collided with the gas pump on the dock. Even though I was angry with Raker and Richard, I was appalled. I hadn't really wanted either of them to die a horrible death. I felt sick. Missy and I were close enough to feel the heat, but not so close that fiery debris fell on us.

It took great skill and finesse to bring the airboat close, but Nick was all right now and ready to meet any challenge. Once we were perched on the seat and had Missy buckled in, I heard a voice calling from the water, "Help me. Over here. Help me," and saw by the light of the moon that Raker clung to a cypress knee not twenty yards away. Nick manipulated the airboat over to him and shut off the motor so we could drift in.

We let the motion of the wake carry us closer and suddenly Raker reached up and grabbed my leg. I screamed as he pulled me off the seat and into the water. I heard Missy holler "Mommy!" as I went under.

When I came up, Raker had let go of my leg, but now he had hold of my hair. I fleetingly thought about getting it cut, but hoped I wouldn't have to deal with this kind of man much longer. He thrashed around in pure panic and I knew that if I didn't do something right away, he could manage to drown us both.

I did what any red-blooded lifeguard would do; I hauled back and hit him in the jaw as hard as I could. It wasn't until then that I recalled Elaine telling me, "The man has a glass jaw!"

She had knocked him out once too ...on the school bus when they were kids. A glass jaw was certainly something else to be thankful for. My hand hurt, but I was able to support him in the water until Nick could haul him into the boat like a big fish. Then he helped me back in and I put my arms around Missy to warm her.

Holding her, I looked at the bright sky and the fire. The whole island seemed to be burning. I thought about the captive birds and sighed for them, but there was nothing I could do.

"Where's Richard?" Nick asked Raker.

"He's gone. He was on the boat the last time I seen him." Raker ran his hand across his eyes. We went around the island as close as we could, searching with the spotlight that somebody had once used for night hunting, but we could find nothing except burned and burning debris. It was so sad.

Richard was a young man with his whole life ahead of him. He might have chosen to trust God. Now it was too late. I knew the only thing I could do for him was to see he got a decent funeral, or at least a memorial. I didn't know who would come, but Missy and I would be there. I wouldn't grieve. The man had made his own choices and he had suffered the natural consequences of them.

No one said anything on the way back. We couldn't hear each other anyway for all the noise the boat made. We were finally together and safe and headed back to Living Spring and home. Raker would see jail time for sure. In addition, Nick, Missy, and I; we would make a family with Hank, Elaine, Bess, Ira, and Annie. Our home would be beautiful and our children would grow up to be fine human beings who loved God and each other.

The End